"I usually don't cotton to demands, but you paid Murphy a lot of cash to fetch me, and that got me curious. What kind of a man pays fifty bucks to a bartender just for running an errand?"

"The kind that is in serious trouble, Mr. Fargo. I have a problem, and I have been advised that you are the man to help me with it."

"Go on."

"Mr. Fargo, some time ago, a certain relic was stolen from . . ." The man looked left, then right, then leaned forward. "You see, I represent a certain European crowned head. Some months ago, against his advisors' express desires, he loaned a certain object to his . . . mistress, for lack of a better term. To make a long story short, she absconded with it and made her way to America, from whence she had come."

"And?" Fargo prompted. "What has this got to do with me?"

"We should like you to track her—and the object. Retrieve it for us."

THE
TRAILSMAN
#252

KANSAS
CITY SWINDLE

by

Jon Sharpe

A SIGNET BOOK

SIGNET
Published by New American Library, a division of
Penguin Putnam Inc., 375 Hudson Street,
New York, New York 10014, U.S.A.
Penguin Books Ltd, 80 Strand,
London WC2R 0RL, England
Penguin Books Australia Ltd, Ringwood,
Victoria, Australia
Penguin Books Canada Ltd, 10 Alcorn Avenue,
Toronto, Ontario, Canada M4V 3B2
Penguin Books (N.Z.) Ltd, 182–190 Wairau Road,
Auckland 10, New Zealand

Penguin Books Ltd, Registered Offices:
Harmondsworth, Middlesex, England

First published by Signet, an imprint of New American Library,
a division of Penguin Putnam Inc.

First Printing, October 2002
10 9 8 7 6 5 4 3 2 1

Copyright © Jon Sharpe, 2002
All rights reserved

The first chapter of this book previously appeared in *Utah Uproar*,
the two hundred fifty-first volume in this series.

 REGISTERED TRADEMARK—MARCA REGISTRADA

Printed in the United States of America

Without limiting the rights under copyright reserved above, no part of
this publication may be reproduced, stored in or introduced into a
retrieval system, or transmitted, in any form, or by any means (electronic,
mechanical, photocopying, recording, or otherwise), without the prior written
permission of both the copyright owner and the above publisher of this
book.

PUBLISHER'S NOTE
This is a work of fiction. Names, characters, places, and incidents either
are the product of the author's imagination or are used fictitiously,
and any resemblance to actual persons, living or dead, events, or locales
is entirely coincidental.

BOOKS ARE AVAILABLE AT QUANTITY DISCOUNTS WHEN USED TO PROMOTE
PRODUCTS OR SERVICES. FOR INFORMATION PLEASE WRITE TO PREMIUM
MARKETING DIVISION, PENGUIN PUTNAM INC., 375 HUDSON STREET, NEW
YORK, NEW YORK 10014.

If you purchased this book without a cover you should be aware that this
book is stolen property. It was reported as "unsold and destroyed"
to the publisher and neither the author nor the publisher has received
any payment for this "stripped book."

The Trailsman

Beginnings . . . they bend the tree and they mark the man. Skye Fargo was born when he was eighteen. Terror was his midwife, vengeance his first cry. Killing spawned Skye Fargo, ruthless, cold-blooded murder. Out of the acrid smoke of gunpowder still hanging in the air, he rose, cried out a promise never forgotten.

The Trailsman they began to call him all across the West: searcher, scout, hunter, the man who could see where others only looked, his skills for hire but not his soul, the man who lived each day to the fullest, yet trailed each tomorrow. Skye Fargo, the Trailsman, the seeker who could take the wildness of a land and the wanting of a woman and make them his own.

Kansas City, 1859—
Thievery may be a sin, but for the most beautiful
of thieves it won't be the first. . . .

1

He had no more than walked out of the night and into the Purple Garter Saloon, dusty and tired from the trail and in dire need of a beer, when a familiar shriek pierced the air.

"Skye Fargo, you old devil!" hollered Rose O'Grady, as she threw herself into his arms from a distance of ten feet.

He caught her, more out of surprise than anything else, but as she wiggled against him, his smile grew to split his face. "Rosie, you old tart! Glad to see you! What in the blue-eyed world are you doin' in Kansas City?"

She slid down to the floor, all five feet two of her, and put her hands on his hips, leaning back just far enough to look up into his face, which gave him a chance to look down her considerable cleavage.

"I might be askin' you the same question, Fargo," she said with a grin that promised he wouldn't be alone tonight. "Where was the last time? Dodge City?"

"I'm thinkin' it was more like Abilene, Rosie," he said, taking her hand and leading her through the crowd toward an empty table.

It was eight o'clock on a Saturday night, and the Purple Garter was smoky and crowded. Through the hum of voices he could hear a roulette wheel spinning and clicking. Tables were crowded with poker players, and the faro table was doing a brisk business, as was the bar.

"Yeah, that's right," she said with a shake of her blonde curls. "Abilene. Frankie Dillinger's place. The Rusty Bucket."

"That's the one." He sank down in a chair, and she sat in the next one after she pulled it around to touch his. "You're lookin' mighty good, Rose," he said. "Hell, you haven't aged a day!"

She hadn't, either. If anything, the five years since they'd met had erased some lines from her face. This struck him as odd for a sporting girl, but more power to her. The hard life usually aged them fast.

"I have had me a whatchacall, Fargo," she said as she held up a hand and signaled to one of the barkeeps for two beers. "'A reversal of fortune,' like they say in the books." She swept her arm wide to take in the whole bar. "Would you believe that I'm the sole proprietor of this whole damn circus?"

Fargo slapped a hand on the scarred table top. "You don't mean to tell me!" he crowed.

She nodded. "You bet your ass, baby. It's mine, lock, stock, and barrel. Four years this October. Ol' Tyrone Clancy left it to me in his will, may he rest in peace." She put a hand over her heart and gazed heavenward, then leaned back and grinned at him. "I'm a lady of property, now."

"Well, I'll be dogged," Fargo said as the bartender brought them their beers. "I'll just be double dogged. That old Tyrone could pinch a five-dollar gold piece till the eagle screamed and flapped its wings. What you figure came over him?"

Rose pointed her index finger and stuck it against her dimpled cheek. She tipped her head and batted the sooty lashes on her pale blue eyes.

Fargo laughed. "Rose, you beat about everything, you know that?"

"I do, Fargo," she said happily. "Yes indeed, I certainly do. So what you been up to?"

Fargo shrugged. "'Bout the same," he said.

She grinned. "Which means that you been saving

folks right and left and havin' adventures all over hell and gone. Same old Fargo."

She took a sip of her beer. "Lord, sometimes I think the whole of the U. S. of A. would just fall right down in a heap if you weren't around to pull our asses out of the fire every five minutes."

He paused, his beer two inches from his lips. He appeared to ponder this. "True, Rosie, too true," he said at last, then broke out in a wide smile.

It was her turn to laugh.

"So what brings you down this way?" she asked at last. "Fire? Flood? Insurrection? A vast and evil plot against the government?" She paused. "Lost dog?"

He laughed. "None of the above," he answered. "I was just down in the Indian Territory on business, and figured to sort of wind my way back out to Colorado. Got a job up in Colorado Springs, but it doesn't start till next month. Thought it might be nice to take it slow for a few weeks." He twirled his beer mug thoughtfully. "Now that I found you, Rose, I might just hang around here for a spell."

She leaned in toward him. "Now, Fargo, that sounds like a real good plan to me." Her hand went to his arm. "Ever since Tyrone left me this place, I been . . . real lonely. The boss lady don't mess with the clients, you know? At least, not when she's got girls to do it for her." She leaned closer. "And as I recall, you and me had us a real good time in Abilene. And in Dodge, too," she purred.

He placed his hand over hers. "You remember right, Rosie," he said softly, and gave her a wink. Had she really gone without for four years? Lord, he was about to have a blue-eyed, dimple-cheeked, pouty-mouthed wild woman on his hands!

It suited him just fine.

Nimble Svenson scuttled down through the Kansas City train yard between the side-railed cars until he found the right one. Looking from side to side, he swung up onto its platform and rapped on the fancy, cut and etched glass panel in the door.

After he'd rapped three times, the brass knob turned and the door opened.

"Yes?" said the man in the shadows. He was big, nearly as big around as he was tall, and a fat cigar jutted from his mouth. He wore a black back-East suit and a silk vest the color of emeralds, and his voice was as deep and sonorous as a death knell.

Nimble swept the hat off his head. "Howdy, M-Mr. Stacy," Nimble said with a smile that was just for show. Stacy made him awfully nervous, if for no other reason than that he was alive. "Mr. Stacy, I think I got the answer to all your problems."

Stacy stared at him for a few seconds, seemed to study on him, which made Nimble all the more anxious. But then Stacy stepped back and opened the door wide. "Come in," he said.

"Sure, yessir, Mr. Stacy," Nimble muttered, and scuttled down the car's narrow hallway in the big man's wake.

Stacy had to duck down just a little, Nimble noticed, and his sides brushed both walls of the little hall. *He'd have a hard pocket to pick,* Nimble thought automatically, and then he brushed the idea from his mind. No more picking pockets, no more badger games, no more trying to find a partner that wouldn't run out on him and take the cash, at least not for a while. This was going to be the night he'd hit the big score.

Unconsciously, he straightened and walked a little taller. Rich. By God, he was going to be a rich man.

Or at least, he'd have some coin in his pocket for a change.

Light hit Nimble in the face as Mr. Stacy suddenly passed into the parlor of the car, leaving Nimble blinking before the lamps, his hat in his hand.

"Tell him," Stacy said, and hiked his thumb toward a new man, one Nimble hadn't met before, who was seated across the little room, a folded newspaper in his lap. From what Nimble could see, the printing sure didn't look like English. A cigar burned in the cut-glass ashtray at his side, although it was longer and thinner than the one clamped in Stacy's teeth.

Nimble looked from the stranger to Stacy and back again.

"It's all right, Mr. Svenson," the man in the chair said. His voice was different from Stacy's, kind of thin and icy, and his accent was strange. Foreign, cultured. He stood up. He was a good bit taller than Nimble, but not so frighteningly tall as Mr. Stacy. A good bit thinner, too. Almost skeletal. He held out a slender hand, and Nimble took it.

"Nimble, if'n you don't mind," Nimble said, his voice cracking a little in the middle. "Everybody calls me that."

The handshake was exceedingly dry and firm, and a sparkling diamond pinkie ring rubbed briefly against Nimble's hand. It took all of Nimble's self-control not to slip it off him.

"Very good. Nimble, then," said the man, smiling slightly. "I am Vladimir Korchenko." He nodded his head in the suggestion of a bow.

"Nice to meetcha, Mr. Korchenko," Nimble said. He was still trying to figure the angle on this. When he'd talked to Stacy before, he'd assumed he was acting alone. Nobody had said anything about some fancy-pants dude from Russia or Hungary or someplace horning in.

Korchenko sat back down and gestured toward the chair opposite his. It was upholstered in red velvet, as was Korchenko's, and looked to be cozy enough and big enough to sleep in. There'd been many a night that Nimble would have paid good money to sleep in a chair like this one.

Nobody had to ask him twice. He sat down. The chair was like a cloud.

"Cigar?" asked Korchenko, and offered a monogrammed silver case from his inside pocket. "Or perhaps you would prefer one of Mr. Stacy's. I find them too harsh, but to each his own."

"Oh no," replied Nimble, and quickly took a cigar. He ran it under his nose. It was a beauty, soaked in cognac if he wasn't mistaken. He stuck it into his pocket and gave it a pat. "This'll be just dandy, and it's right nice of you. I'll just save it for later on, if'n you don't mind."

Korchenko lifted a brow, but that was all. He closed the case with a click and replaced it. "Certainly, Nimble, certainly," he said, and leaned back. He picked up his cigar, rolled the ash off against the side of the ashtray, and took a puff. "You have news for us? You have found our man?"

Nimble nodded. "I sure have. Just the right feller, too." He eyed Korchenko's brandy snifter, which he'd just spotted.

"Franklin?" Korchenko said to Stacy. "A glass for our friend."

Franklin Stacy, then. This put a whole new twist on the deal. Korchenko looked to be the boss of Stacy. At least, Nimble was pretty sure of it, since Stacy hadn't perched once since they came in, and now Stacy was at the little bar, pouring out Nimble's drink. And all the time he'd figured that Stacy was the man in charge.

Nimble slouched back and slung his elbow over the arm of the chair. Pretty damned grand, if you asked him. And he had what they needed. The catbird seat, that's what he was in!

Stacy handed him a snifter, and Nimble swirled it under his nose, aping an actor he'd seen in a play one time.

"Real nice, Mr. Korchenko," he said, and he meant it. It was all he could do to keep from chugging down the brandy and asking for more, it was that good. As it was, he took just a sip. It rolled over his tongue and down his throat, smooth as heated honey.

Nimble looked around the car. Cut-glass lamps, nice paintings of horses and hounds and such, rich paneling, lots of gilt, and deep plush carpets. He remembered the *"VK"* etched into the glass of the back door, where he'd come in. They didn't rent out Pullman cars this nice, not with a man's own initials cut into them. Korchenko must own it.

"You fellers have got you a real class operation, here," Nimble said with an approving nod. "Yessir, real class."

"Thank you, Nimble," Korchenko said with another of those bow-nods. "I am so pleased that you approve. And now, who and where is this gentleman whom you have found for us?"

"You boys ever heard of a feller called Skye Fargo?" Nimble asked, swirling his brandy again. He was feeling rather full of himself. And to think he'd had to work up the courage to come looking for Stacy!

Korchenko furrowed his brow and looked at Stacy. Stacy came forward a step and said, "I have, Vladimir." And then he turned to Nimble and arched a brow. "You have found Skye Fargo for us? Here? In Kansas City?"

That "us" sort of bothered Nimble. Shouldn't Stacy have said that he'd found him for Korchenko?

But he said, "Yessir, I sure have. Course, him and me ain't personally acquainted, but I reckon he's just the man you're lookin' for. Couldn't find no better, I'll wager."

Korchenko looked up at Stacy. "You know this man?"

"Only by reputation, Vladimir," Stacy said. "They call him the Trailsman. He is a tall man, I've heard, and conversant in several tongues including those of the natives. He led the Castlerock party through the wilderness, and single-handedly put an outlaw called Little Tommy Scraggs—and this was a fellow who had murdered seven men—on the gallows."

"Scraggs?" said Korchenko with arched brows and a shake of his head. "These Americans have such colorful names."

"He also whipped the R&G Railroad boys," piped up Nimble, who was nearly finished with his brandy. "Caught Sammy Fishback dead to rights, broke up

7

that big strike on the Dead Ringer mine out in California, and I hear he put the kibosh on some big bank swindle up in Montana, too, and went undercover to do it. Oh, he's a slick one, and he's got guts. Always heard tell that them blue eyes of his could slice right through you, and havin' seem 'em for myself tonight, I'm believin' they're right."

Nimble slid a long glance toward the bar and the decanter. It looked to him like they could afford to give a poor fellow another glass of welcome. "Could I talk you into pourin' me another, Mr. Stacy?" He held out his snifter.

Stacy took it, although he didn't budge in the direction of the bar. "That's correct, Vladimir," he said. To Nimble, he asked, "And he is here? In Kansas City?"

"Yessir, he sure is," Nimble said. He could practically feel the rumble of Stacy's voice through his shoes, even when the man was talking in a conversational tone.

"Right across town at the Purple Garter Saloon," Nimble continued. "I heard him tellin' Miss Rose that he was at loose ends till next month. Reckon you could get him, all right. Reckon you could get him easy. For whatever it is you want him for." He eyed his brandy glass once more, as it dangled in Stacy's fingers.

"More brandy for our friend," said Korchenko, and Stacy finally went to the bar.

"Thank you, sir," said a relieved Nimble. That was the best brandy he'd ever had, even better than they'd served at the fancy hotel in Chicago where Eva-Marie Sutcliffe had stolen all his money. The goddamn bitch. "Now, about the payment . . ."

Korchenko held up a finger. "In time, Nimble, in time. Where is this Fargo staying?"

Nimble shrugged. "Right upstairs from the bar, far as I could tell." He grinned suddenly, and rather smarmily. "Sounded like him and Miss Rose was old friends, if'n you know what I mean." He winked at Korchenko knowingly. "You can't miss him. Slim feller. Got him a close-cropped beard and he wears these old bucks."

Korchenko cocked a brow. "Bucks?"

"Buckskin," Stacy explained. "Deerhide. Fringed, like some of the native tribes wear."

"That's right," said Nimble, nodding. "They got fringe on 'em, all right."

"Very good, very good," said Korchenko, at the same moment that Stacy handed Nimble his second brandy. "I believe you and Mr. Stacy had already agreed on a finder's fee? Five hundred dollars, was it not?"

Just the mention of all that money jarred Nimble— but in a happy way, of course—and he downed the brandy in one gulp. A welcome warmth spread through his belly. "Yessir," he said. "That was . . . uh . . . the figure mentioned."

"Mr. Stacy?" said Korchenko.

Without ceremony, Stacy dropped a small bag of coins into Nimble's lap. He also took his brandy glass.

Nimble opened the bag, but before he could pour the coins out and have a real look at all that money, Korchenko added, "Half now, half if he agrees to do the work."

Nimble peered into the bag. Damn it, Korchenko was right. Only two hundred and fifty.

Nimble pulled the drawstring again. "How'll I know?" he asked, and this time, emboldened by brandy, he didn't pretend to smile. "I mean, what's to keep you fellers from skippin' town on me?"

Korchenko stood up. "You have merely my word, Nimble. But I assure you, it is as constant as the North star."

Oh, what the hell, thought Nimble. Stacy had put out feelers with several of the fellows in town, and he had happened to come up with somebody good— somebody great—right off the bat, and brought the name to them before anybody else. Hell's bells, he'd come up with the one and only Skye Fargo!

Even if Stacy and Korchenko did skip, at least he

was two hundred and fifty bucks richer than he'd been a few minutes ago. And besides, what if Fargo said no to whatever they were planning? He couldn't help that, could he? Of course not!

Besides, he wasn't about to step outside with that fancy-tailored bruiser, Stacy, and fight for the rest of his money, no sir! Stacy could likely bash in his skull with just one finger.

"Okay," Nimble said, and stuck the little pouch in his pocket. "Whatever you say."

"Excellent," said Korchenko, and smiled. His face reminded Nimble of one of those waxwork dummies he'd seen when he was in San Francisco.

"If Mr. Fargo agrees," Korchenko went on, "Mr. Stacy will find you and pay you the balance of your fee. You have no need to worry. Of course, if there is no Mr. Fargo extant, if you have simply brought us a tale with no substance, Mr. Stacy will be collecting the payment he just gave you."

Nimble gulped. He hoped they didn't notice. "Oh, there's a Fargo, all right. Big as life and tough as nails."

Stacy set his brandy snifter on the bar and clasped his hands behind his back. "You will be in the usual place, Mr. Svenson?" he asked flatly.

"The usual place, yeah," said Nimble. His usual place was in the back room of the Addington Bar, where he was currently running a craps game.

Nobody had ever accused Nimble of not knowing when to leave, and seeing as how everybody was up except him, he rose, too.

"Sure, Mr. Korchenko, sure," he said as affably as he could. That Fargo feller better not skip town any-time soon, or Nimble's ass would be grass. "Nice working with you."

This time he stuck out his hand first, and Korchenko took it. His hand was as dry and cool as talcum pow-der. Talcum-powdered wax, Nimble thought, and shuddered.

"Mr. Stacy will find me," he repeated.

2

By the time nine o'clock rolled around, Fargo and Rose were upstairs, and Fargo was slipping his fingers beneath the final layers of Rose's petticoats, looking for the ties.

He'd already bared her to the waist, and her breasts were as glorious as he remembered: round, full, and milky-white, with large, upturned nipples the color of seashells. At present, they were puckered with desire.

"Hurry, Fargo," she breathed. Her yellow hair had lost most of its pins, and hung down over her smooth, creamy shoulders.

"I am, baby, I am," he whispered, and paused to take her lips again. Her mouth was soft and welcoming, although a little urgent.

He was as anxious as she was. He'd been hard as a rock since they mounted the first stair step.

Just as his fingers freed the knot, somebody rapped at the door. Both he and Rose ignored it. He scooped her up, naked, into his arms, paused to tease a nipple with his tongue, and started for the bed.

The knocking came again, this time more insistent.

"Go away!" Rose called, over his shoulder.

Fargo put her down on the sheets.

"Come closer, you lovely, darling man," she whispered.

The knocking turned to pounding. "Miss Rose?" called a male voice. "Miss Rose!"

Placing a hand against Fargo's chest, Rose closed

her eyes, then called, "What the hell do you want, Murphy? We're kind of busy in here."

"Sorry, Miss Rose," Murphy shouted back, through the door. "But there's a duded-up feller downstairs, says he's gotta speak to Mr. Fargo real urgentlike."

"Tell him later," Fargo shouted, and nipped at Rose's ear.

"Says it can't wait," Murphy shouted. He paused, then added, "He said he'd pay me fifty bucks if I could bring you down real fast, Mr. Fargo. Please?"

Even Rose blinked at that comment. "That's more than I pay Murphy in a month," she said, craning her neck toward the door. "Now, who the hell . . ."

"Suppose I'd best go find out," Fargo said, after he hollered much the same thing at Murphy, and reluctantly stood up and began slithering into his britches. He glanced back at Rose, who lay there naked and inviting, albeit with a rather quizzical look on her face.

"Hold that pose, Rosie," he said. "And that thought. I'll be back."

With one sweep of her dainty arm, she pulled up the covers. Holding them under her chin, she said, "You'd better be, baby."

Fargo walked down the stairs and immediately saw the man who'd requested an interview. There was no mistaking him.

He was almost a giant, and his wide backside, heavy with fat, sagged ominously over both sides of the wooden barroom chair. Clean-shaven, immaculately groomed, and dressed in a black suit tailored to make the best of his bulk, he sat alone at a table in the rear. His hat and gloves were placed neatly at his side, an untouched whiskey sat before him, and when another patron walked too close to the back of his chair, he leaned out of the way so as to avoid being touched.

It struck Fargo that he looked just about as comfortable as a Boston Brahmin invited to tea in a leper colony.

Fargo was halfway to the table when the gentleman in question stood up and nodded his head in a bow.

"Skye Fargo, I presume?" he asked in a deep, melodious voice that matched his size.

Fargo nodded. "And you are?"

"Franklin Q. Stacy, at your service, sir," he said, and offered a meaty hand. Fargo shook it, and they sat down.

Fargo was glad of it. When Stacy was standing, he made Fargo feel like a midget. He figured the man's height to be at least six feet six, and he'd dance a jig naked in the street if Stacy weighed less than three hundred and fifty pounds.

"What can I do for you, Mr. Stacy?" Fargo asked. "And make it quick. I was kind of busy when I got your demand."

Stacy sat back just a hair. "It wasn't meant to be a demand, sir. Quite the contrary."

"Came across that way," Fargo said. "I usually don't cotton to demands, but you paid Murphy a lot of cash to fetch me, and that sorta got me curious. What kind of a man pays fifty bucks to a bartender just for runnin' an errand?"

"The kind that is in serious trouble, Mr. Fargo," Stacy replied, steepling his fingertips. "I have a problem, and I have been advised that you are the man to help me with it."

"I'm mildly curious, Mr. Stacy," said Fargo, and waved at Murphy, who was hovering nearby. "Beer," he said, and Murphy disappeared into the crowd. "Go on," he said to Stacy.

"Mr. Fargo, some time ago, a certain relic was stolen from . . ." Stacy looked left, then right, then leaned forward, across the table. "Can you assure me that anything I tell you will be held in the strictest confidence?"

Fargo nodded. "Of course. My word on it."

Stacy was looking a tad nervous, and Fargo was intrigued.

"You want me to swear on a Bible?" he asked.

"No, no. Not necessary," said Stacy, producing a monogrammed handkerchief, with which he mopped his brow. "I understand you to be a man of honor, Mr. Fargo, as am I. You see, I represent a certain European crowned head. Some months ago, against his advisors' express desires, he loaned a certain . . . object to his mistress, for lack of a better term. To make a long story short, she absconded with it and made her way to America, from whence she had come."

"And?" Fargo prompted when Stacy paused. "What has this got to do with me?"

"We should like to hire you to track her—and the object," Stacy said, all in a rush. "Retrieve it for us."

"Seems to me you should have gone to the Pinkertons," Fargo said. Murphy brought him his beer, and he took a sip. "They'd be your best bet. Allan Pinkerton and his boys take care of things like this all the time."

But Stacy made a face. "No, no, Mr. Fargo," he said. "The delicacy of this matter is most imperative. We cannot go to Allan Pinkerton. We cannot take the slightest chance that any breath of this foul business will ever come to public scrutiny."

Fargo cocked his head. "I don't get it, Mr. Stacy. Why not?"

Stacy leaned farther forward. "Because what this gutter snipe has stolen, Mr. Fargo, is half of the crown jewels, in the form of fifty perfect diamonds, four large flawless rubies, and a handful of Kashmir sapphires, all set in a tiara of the purest gold. In short, she has stolen the—"

"The Moldavian Crown?" Fargo said.

Stacy blinked rapidly, then moped at his forehead again.

"Don't go getting your knickers in a twist, Stacy," Fargo said. "We're not so far removed out here as you might think. I saw that crown in the papers about a year ago. As I recall, they said it only gets taken out once a year for some state event. How'd she get her hands on it, anyway? I mean, how'd she talk him into it? Whoever he is. Whoever *she* is." He wished Stacy would start throwing names at him.

"Matters of the heart, Mr. Fargo. Matters of the heart," said Stacy with a shake of his head. "Who can tell what runs through a man's mind when he thinks he is in love?"

Fargo lifted a brow.

"The point is," continued Stacy, "that she most assuredly has it, and we believe her to be a very sly operator indeed. If I were to go anywhere near her, she would most certainly shy far away. You, on the other hand . . ."

"You want me to steal it back, is that it?"

Stacy nodded. "Precisely."

"Don't suppose you've got any idea where she is?"

"Oh, that I do," Stacy said. "She is on her way to Lincoln, Nebraska, where I believe she has friends. She is stopping there en route to San Francisco."

Fargo said, "You're going to have to tell me her name, friend. Or is that a state secret, too?"

Stacy reached into a pocket and produced a small leather picture holder, the kind that opens like a book, which he proceeded to fan open. He held it out and Fargo took it.

Fargo whistled long and low.

She was beautiful. Slender, light-haired, light-eyed, and dressed to the nines, she had fine features and full lips, perhaps a little too full for fashion, but what the hell. Her hair was piled atop her head in a million soft curls, her jawline was clean but soft and womanly, her throat like a swan's, her decolletage enticing.

"Yes, indeed," Stacy said, responding to Fargo's whistle. "Her name is Francesca Ponti, an American of Italian extraction." He pointed to the picture. "And that hair is red, by the way. Her eyes are green. She presented herself as a well-bred lady of some consequence. We were all taken in, I'm afraid. However, we have since learned it was all a ruse, a ruse to get her close enough to the jewels to . . ."

"Swipe them," Fargo said.

"I warn you, Mr. Fargo," Stacy said, suddenly stern. "Do not take this lightly. Francesca Ponti is very clever, and just as deadly. A royal guard was found dead in her wake."

Fargo considered this. He closed the picture case and sat back, twirling his beer. "How much?" he asked. "Provided I can catch up with her and get the bauble back for you."

"Five thousand," Stacy said without batting an eye.

Fargo's brow furrowed. "Dollars?"

"Dollars," Stacy said. "One half of which is to be paid upon your agreeing to take the matter into hand, and the remaining half upon delivery of the item. We do not care what you do with Miss Ponti."

Fargo considered this for a moment. Then he said, "Stacy, how'd you get mixed up in this? You're an American, far as I can tell. You've got no accent, anyhow."

"A good question," Stacy said, and at last took a sip of the whiskey before him. He made a face, then pushed the glass away. "Wretched," he muttered before lifting his head again. "I am simply the American contact for the gentleman from which the item was stolen, Mr. Fargo. I am a diplomat. Of sorts. I act as his liaison."

"You said 'we' before."

"Yes," Stacy said with a nod. "I speak of my, uh, partner. Vladimir Korchenko. You will be dealing with me exclusively, however."

"I see. And when's this tiara scheduled to be shown to the public again?" Fargo asked, remembering the article.

"On Christmas Day," said Stacy, "according to tradition. We simply must have it back by the first of November to get it safely home in time for the ceremony."

Fargo twirled his beer mug again. This was the middle of September. If he couldn't track it down in a month and a half, it couldn't be tracked.

He looked up at Stacy. "All right. I'll get your doodad." After all, how much trouble could that little gal in the picture be? Stacy said she'd killed a man, but then, he had decided that Stacy was a little too predisposed to theatricality.

Stacy's face broadened into a smile. "Splendid, Mr. Fargo, just splendid." He reached into a pocket and brought out a fat envelope, then pushed it across the table. "We have a deal, then."

Fargo slid the envelope into his bucks without opening it. He lifted his mug. "Let's drink to it," he said.

Stacy made a face. "Must we?" he asked, but raised his whiskey anyway.

Back upstairs, Fargo found Rose O'Grady scantily clad in a pale-green, see-through negligee which put all her marvels on a deliciously hazy display. She was posed in the middle of that big bed of hers, but she wasn't smiling.

Far from it.

"What the hell took you so long?" was the first thing out of her mouth.

Well, like the man said, you could catch more flies with honey than with vinegar. Fargo smiled and sat down in a chair opposite the bed, and began to pull off his boots.

"Got a job, baby," he said. "Going to be big money for practically no work."

"So?" she said.

"So, I know a certain blonde-headed gal that used to admire yellow dresses and big, fancy hats," he said. "Remember her?"

A smile crept over Rose's face. "You bet I do, darlin'. What's the job?"

His boots off, he stood up and tugged off his leather shirt, not bothering with the laces. He was in a hurry.

"Been sworn to secrecy, Rosie," he said. "But I've

got the down payment." He picked up his discarded shirt, pulled the envelope from its pocket, and tossed it over to her.

She caught it and gave him a curious look.

"Go ahead, Rose," he said, working at his britches. "Open it."

He heard paper ripping as he skinned out of his pants, and by the time he joined her on the bed, naked, she was fanning twenty-five one hundred dollar bills, all in new currency, in her pretty fingers.

Eyes wide, she said, "This is just the down payment? Fargo, you old buzzard, you've been holding out on me! I thought you just saved the world every hour on the hour because you were so good natured!"

"Hell, no, Rosie," he said with a grin, and pushed her back on the bed. "At heart, I'm a mercenary son of a bitch."

She opened her hand and the bills fluttered to the sheets.

"Tell me more," she said before she kissed him.

Fargo took her there and then, making love to her on a satisfying bed of cash. She was just as smooth, just as soft as the last time, and just as fiery. She squirmed against him, teasing him with her inner muscles, meeting him thrust for thrust. He drove into her, slow at first, then fast and hard until, both slick with sweat, they climaxed together.

They lay there quietly for a moment, catching their breath and panting, and Rose idly scooped up a couple of hundred dollar bills.

"Hallelujah," she said softly.

"What?" said Fargo, a smile teasing at the corners of his mouth.

Rose smiled back. "Not only have I got a prize bull in my bed, he's rich to boot. I think that deserves a hallelujah, don't you?"

He propped himself up on one elbow and rested his palm on her belly. Then he kissed one pink nipple. "I think that deserves two, Rosie."

She cocked her head against the pillow. "Already, Fargo?" she asked coyly. "You made of steel?"

"Nope," he said with a grin. "Just awful eager flesh."

Her hand slipped down to his member, and she wrapped her fingers around him. "No, steel it is," she said softly. She grinned when he felt himself swell even more against her grip. "Why, land sakes, Fargo! I didn't know you cared so much."

"That's just the beginning, Rosie," he whispered into her ear.

Nimble Svenson was taking a break from his craps game, and was just coming back from the outhouse, out back. He paused to take a long look down the alley. It seemed to him that Stacy should have contacted him by now. After all, he had got the feeling that he and that Korchenko character were in a hurry.

Boy, oh, boy, he hoped that Skye Fargo wouldn't fly the coop before they talked to him! That would be the topper, wouldn't it, if Stacy came and asked for his money back?

He walked through the dark to the back door of the saloon and was just about to open it when a familiar voice said his name.

"Mr. Svenson?"

"Nimble," he corrected automatically, and then he brightened, recognizing the voice. "Oh, how do, Mr. Stacy. You fellers talk to Fargo already?" he added hopefully, and squinted into the shadows. He still couldn't see Stacy. Where the hell was he?

As if Nimble had spoken his thoughts, Stacy stepped into the dim light. How a great big fellow like that could hide to the point where he was almost invisible was beyond Nimble.

"You got talent, Mr. Stacy," he said to hide his surprise.

"Thank you, Nimble," Stacy answered. "And to answer your question, yes, I've been to see Mr. Fargo. He will do quite nicely."

"Good, good," said Nimble eagerly. He felt his head bobbing a little too enthusiastically, and stopped it. "You come to pay me off, have you?"

"That I have," said Stacy, and reached into his pocket. He began to dig about in it. "On behalf of Mr. Korchenko and myself, I should like to thank you, Nimble. You have been most helpful."

Nimble had gone from excited to worried in the blink of an eye. Stacy continued to fumble in his pocket and, a little out of sorts, Nimble said, "What'd you do, forget to bring my money?"

"Certainly not," said Stacy, who appeared to find what he was searching for. "I assure you, I didn't forget a thing."

His hand came forward from under his jacket, toward Nimble's outstretched palm, and just before it reached him, a blade flashed from Stacy's fist.

Before Nimble could react, Stacy drove the blade forward, striking upward through Nimble's coat and vest and then twisting into his ribs. Nimble had the odd thought that now he knew what a piked fish felt like, and then he fell.

Crumpled was really what he did. He folded up on the spot and fell in a heap at Stacy's feet, slipping off the blade as he went down.

"There, there, Nimble," Stacy muttered as he quickly went through Nimble's pockets and found the little leather bag of coins. Nimble watched, blurrily, as Stacy stood up, hefted the bag in his palm, then stuck it in his coat pocket before he bent to wipe his knife's blade on Nimble's coat.

"My money," Nimble said, but it came out breathy, barely understandable. His arms didn't seem to work, nor his legs. He felt warmth spreading over his midsection. Funny, but there wasn't any pain. Everything just felt heavy, so heavy. Maybe it was time he went to sleep.

"No," corrected Stacy. "My money. It was always my money."

Stacy snapped the blade closed again and stuck it

into his pocket. He regarded Nimble, who by now was able to see his attacker only as a fuzzy, formless thing hovering over him in the shadows.

Nimble tried to stay, "You lousy son of a bitch." Even he couldn't understand what came out, though.

Stacy was still looking at him, as if he were waiting for him to die. And then, quite abruptly, he said, "Dear me, I seem to have broken your heart. Put quite a sizable hole in it, anyway." He grinned. "No need to dirty my blade again."

And then he tipped his hat, bowed slightly, and said, "Good night and God's speed, Nimble Svenson. You have proved most useful."

His shiny black shoes were still echoing down the alley when Nimble's world went dark.

3

By nine o'clock the next morning, Fargo had partaken
of a monster of a breakfast (served up by Rose's cook,
in Rose's kitchen), bade Rose a teary good-bye (tem-
porarily, of course, and the tears were hers), made
arrangements at the local livery for his horse, the
Ovaro, and was standing on the station platform,
checking his pocket watch.

The train was late. As usual.

He figured to ride the rails up to Lincoln, track
down Francesca Ponti, steal back the tiara, and be
back inside the week. Her picture was in his pocket,
and what man, having once seen her, could fail to
recognize her?

That was a lucky thing, her being such a beauty.
She was likely to cause heads to turn in every single
place she went.

No, she wasn't one to fade into a crowd, or to pass
unnoticed. She'd be easy as pie to track.

He tried out this theory on the first porter that
passed his seat, once the train finally arrived and he
got going.

"You seen this lady?" he asked, pulling out the
tintype.

It was a hundred-to-one shot, but low and behold,
the porter's brows hiked a good half inch. He was a
big, blond, beefy Swede, with clean features and eyes
that were none too bright.

"That red-headed lady!" he said with a broad grin and an implied wink. "Sure, I remember her." And then the man's face darkened. "Say, what you want with her, anyhow?"

That last comment said a paragraph and a half to Fargo.

It told him that while the porter wasn't above a little idle speculation about his own chances with the fair Francesca, he felt protective of her.

It told him that she'd been kind rather than remote, warm rather than cold, but just standoffish enough to promote worship—for lack of a better term—rather than out-and-out lust.

It told him that he'd better say something fast if he didn't want to get his clock punched instead of his ticket.

He slipped the picture back into his pocket. "She's my cousin," he said, thinking fast. "My cousin Francesca. Beautiful, isn't she?"

A smile returned to the porter's face. "She surely is that. An awful nice lady, too," he added, reinforcing Fargo's thoughts about the standoffish part.

And then the porter looked Fargo up and down, took in the buckskins and the beard and the guns and the Arkansas toothpick strapped to his leg, and, with a cocked brow, asked, "You related by blood, mister?"

"No, no," replied Fargo hurriedly, and shrugged. "She married my second cousin, William. The Boston branch of the family."

The glower returned. "She said it was 'Miss'."

"Oh, it was a secret marriage," Fargo said quickly. He looked up and down the aisle most theatrically, then leaned toward the porter.

"Don't mention that I said anything, all right?" he whispered. "It's just that, well, I'm so damned proud to have a classy filly like her in the family, even if it isn't my branch of it. She's out here visiting some relatives, and I just couldn't help myself. I have to go and meet this gal."

Fargo winked, and the porter's face relaxed. "Sure," he said. "Sure, buddy. Your cousin sure is one lucky man. Ticket?"

Fargo handed it over.

He had best get himself some new clothes when he got up into Nebraska, Fargo thought as he leaned back in his seat. There was no one sitting across the way, so he put his long legs up and got comfortable. Yes, he'd best outfit himself like somebody from back East, or at least the more rustic Kansas City. That would likely make her feel more inclined to trust him. He'd get himself a bowler hat and a collar and studs and everything.

The idea of that scratchy collar sent a shudder through him, but five thousand dollars was five thousand dollars. He could put up with a little itch for five thousand, couldn't he? And besides, he could surely afford it.

Franklin Stacy's roll made a happy bulge in his pocket.

He folded his arms over his chest and watched the Kansas landscape roll by.

Francesca Ponti stepped down onto the platform of the Lincoln depot and batted dust and cinders from her cloak.

Filthy trains. And she'd have to put up with them for a little while longer before she'd feel really truly safe.

She hadn't seen anyone remotely suspicious on the train—no one with an Eastern European accent, no one with impeccable manners and questioning eyes—and nobody had loitered near her.

"Let's keep it that way," she muttered.

"Yoo-hoo!" a voice called. "Franny! Over here!"

Francesca put on her best smile before she turned toward the voice. She raised a gloved hand and waved at the little blonde woman who had hailed her.

"Mae!" she cried happily, and quite honestly, too. "Oh, Mae, dearest! I'm so glad to see you!"

Mae Purvis ran forward, threw her arms about Francesca's shoulders—this was quite a stretch for Mae, who was barely five feet tall—and hugged her close.

"Franny, darling, it's been simply ages!" she said, and tears welled in her eyes. She held Francesca at arm's length. "Oh, my God! You don't look a day older than the last time I saw you, Franny. How do you do that?"

Francesca laughed. "And you look five years younger than I, you minx," she said.

"Don't horseshit me, Franny," Mae said, her sparkling brown eyes bubbling with enthusiasm as well as tears. She pulled out a hanky and dabbed at them. "I been around the track plenty of times."

"My dear Mae," said Francesca as she bent to pick up her bag, "I *am* the race course."

Laughing, Mae scooped up the other bag. "Law," she said as they started down the platform, "I have surely missed you. You decide on how long you can stay? I'm hopin' you'll stay just forever. Plenty of fat purses in this town to go around, and I figure you'll take more than your share. Hell, you could come out of Lincoln stinking rich!"

Francesca shrugged. "I'd adore to, Mae, but I've got to get on to San Francisco. Business. You understand, don't you, Mae? I'd very much like to stay over for a few days, though."

"Well, I'll take what you can spare," Mae said. "And you can bet that I'll keep on tryin' to talk you into it. You got trunks?"

Francesca nodded. "I had them sent ahead to your place."

Mae sniffed and shook her head. "Probably already there. Nobody tells me anything."

They stepped down off the platform, and Francesca followed Mae toward a line of standing wagons and rigs. Heads turned as they approached.

"Good thing," said Mae. "I only brought the buggy. There it is." She pointed down the row and waved her hankie. "Tommy!"

A dark-haired youth, leaning against the side of a shiny black buggy, suddenly came to attention, and upon seeing Francesca, swept off his hat.

"Holy shit!" he mouthed.

"Enough of that, you lecherous little scamp," Mae scolded, although only half-heartedly, as they walked up to meet him. "Tommy, this is my friend, Francesca Ponti. Miss Ponti to you. She'll be staying with us for a few days."

"Holy cow," breathed Tommy, who simply stood there, blinking up at Francesca.

Francesca was accustomed to this reaction from men of all ages and sizes. She was, after all, taller than most—five-feet-ten in her stockinged feet—and she always wore heels. She had come to accept that she was a very striking woman. She had more than accepted it. She'd played on it for years. Looking down on men from her height, she must appear as a goddess, or so she'd been told on numerous occasions.

The idiots.

Acting as if nothing were out of the ordinary, she stepped forward and extended her hand. "I am so very pleased to meet you, Tommy."

Numbly, he took it, but didn't shake it, simply held it and stared up hopelessly into her eyes. "M-Miss Ponti," he finally managed.

"Down, boy, down," said a weary Mae, and physically extricated Francesca's hand. "Bags?" She had to snap her fingers a few times in front of his face. "Tommy! Wake up! Bags."

"Uh, oh yeah," he mumbled, and finally tore his gaze away.

"Moron," Mae mumbled as she and Francesca climbed into the buggy seat. "Sorry about that," she whispered behind her glove. "I forgot what it's like to be around you. But it's your own fault, you know. If you weren't so damned drop-dead gorgeous . . ."

"Now, Mae," said Francesca tiredly. She'd heard this before, too, from countless other women.

"Well, I suppose you've learned to accept these things . . ." Mae continued, then added, "My God, you could make a bloody fortune here, Franny! A king's ransom!"

"With a manager's fee to you, of course," Francesca said with a wink. "I know your game, your mercenary little minx."

"There is that," Mae said, and straightened her skirts. "Tommy!" she shouted. "Are those damn bags secured yet?"

Francesca chuckled at this, and settled her hand over one of Mae's. "Same old Mae," she said softly.

A little over half an hour later, Francesca was unpacking her trunks in Mae's spare room. It wasn't really a spare room, though. Little touches showed signs of recent habitation, most likely by one of Mae's girls. Francesca briefly wondered where the previous inhabitant was spending her nights, then shrugged it off. Whoever she was, it wouldn't hurt her to spend a couple of nights roughing it on the sofa.

The house was in one of the trendier parts of Lincoln, from what Francesca could tell. There weren't any drunks leaning in doorways, there were no girls on the street hawking their wares, and everybody seemed to be reasonably well dressed.

This was a great relief to Francesca, who had wanted to stay in a nice, quiet hotel, until Mae had pestered her into staying with her. Francesca had been worried that she'd have to stay in some flea trap of a whorehouse on the wrong side of town.

But Mae seemed to be doing very well for herself. A nice address, a nice house (even if the decor was on the gauche side), and some high-class girls, from what Francesca had seen.

It was too bad that Mae had so little taste, though. She could have used Francesca's help in that area.

She should get rid of these horrid old carpets, for instance, and replace them with something more modern. And she really should do something about the decor downstairs! Too much gilt, to many ornate details, and the chairs were too small. And pink! It made Francesca dizzy!

Shiny brass and glass, that was what was called for, and more deep leather chairs, more sporting prints, more subdued colors, and lower lighting. Everything should be sleek, simple, comfortable, and big, appealing to a more manly eye and a man's taste.

Well, Mae never did understand that whoring was supposed to appeal to the men on every single level, not just the part with the naked girl.

Oh, well.

Shrugging, Francesca at last came to her gowns. She wasn't going to unpack them, not by a long shot. Where on earth would there be in Lincoln, Nebraska, that called for them, anyway?

But she found one particular dress, a heavy green formal gown, all silk and satin and tulle net, and paused to stroke it. She smiled, then shifted and turned it until she found the bustle. Lifting it, her fingers probed, then found what she was looking for.

She felt the outline of the tiara, sewn beneath layers of padding. It was still there.

She was tempted to slit the seam, just to look at it again. Just to hold it.

So pretty.

So expensive.

So . . . hers.

She grinned.

Mae wanted her to stay on in Lincoln. To make her fortune there.

"If you only knew, Mae," she whispered as she stood up and closed the trunk. "King's ransom, indeed!"

4

With an eye to the prize he had to steal and then bring all the way back to Kansas City, Fargo had picked himself up a new suit of clothes in Omaha. He drew the line at checks and plaids, though. He held out, instead, for a plain brown three-piece rig that was neither so mousy that he faded into nothing, nor so loud that he looked like a damned perfume drummer.

He ended up not getting himself a bowler hat, though. Instead, he chose a simple brown Stetson, the same hue as the suit.

He changed on the train, rolling his buckskins up tight and putting them in his worn—and borrowed—valise, next to his other set. He was glad he'd bought the suit coat just a little too big. That way his sidearms didn't bulge out and call attention to themselves.

Although, he thought, what use would he find for a sidearm? His quarry was, after all, a lady. Quite a lady, by the looks of her. Stacy had claimed otherwise, but what Stacy claimed and what Fargo's instincts told him were two different things.

Still, better to be safe than sorry.

Long before they were scheduled to pull into the Lincoln depot, Fargo looked as common as the next pilgrim—the next pilgrim in a beard, anyhow. There was no way in Hades that he'd shave it off.

He got into a poker game with two farmers, a rube, and a button-and-notions drummer, and by the time the porter came around, calling, "Lincoln, Nebraska, next stop!" he had collected quite a sizable pot: enough to cover his new clothes and some besides.

He was in a very good mood, indeed, when he stepped down onto the platform.

He asked around, and finally found a man, a hack driver, who had seen the fair Francesca.

"You think I could forget somebody what looks like that?" the man said incredulously. He whistled long and low, and was loathe to hand the tintype back to Fargo. "Lordie, Lordie."

"When'd she get in?" Fargo asked, pocketing the picture.

"Yesterday, 'bout noon," replied the cabby. He patted his horse's hip, then hiked a brow. "Why you askin', anyhow?"

Fargo leaned closer and winked conspiratorially. "I miss her," he whispered.

Fargo had taken the right tack, because the cabby grinned back at him smarmily. "I can sure see why," he said.

"Got any idea where she went?" Fargo asked.

"Hell, yeah," said the driver. "I know exactly."

It was Fargo's turn to raise a brow.

The driver grinned. "Miss Mae picked her up, big as life. Acted like they was old friends. Yeah, I know just exactly where they went off to. Me and old Floss, here, will take you there for two bits."

"Deal," said Fargo, and climbed into the buggy.

Old Floss and the cabby, whose name turned out to be Willie Simmons, took Fargo through town. On the trip he learned that it was rumored that Lincoln was about to be named the new state capitol—which accounted for all the new construction and hubbub— and that Miss Mae was the notorious proprietor of the Purvis House, Lincoln's finest brothel.

This put a whole new twist on Francesca Ponti. Her close friend, as Willie had described Miss Mae, was a soiled dove? Chances were, Francesca hadn't fallen far from the sisterly tree.

My, my, thought Fargo. *Not only a comely thief,*

but one that's for sale. He was growing a whole new admiration for Francesca Ponti.

They wound into a nice part of town, and Willie stopped the buggy before a three-story, clapboard building painted white with pink-and-violet trim. There were no gaudy signs outside advertising the wares, just a small one at the gate that simply said, "Purvis."

"This be the place," Willie announced. When Fargo just sat there, making no attempt to get down to the ground, he added, "Um, you need some help with that satchel, Mister?"

Fargo scratched at the back of his neck. He couldn't just walk in and demand Francesca turn over the tiara, could he?

He said, "Where's the nearest hotel?"

"Just up the street," Willie replied, and pointed. "The Washington Arms. Hell, you can throw a rock and hit it from here."

Fargo sat back and crossed his arms. "Might as well ride," he said.

"Kind of expensive in there," Willie warned.

"Not a problem."

Willie shrugged and clucked to Flossie.

Back at the Lincoln depot, Vladimir Korchenko's private Pullman was just being eased onto a side railing. The car came to a halt rather abruptly, and Korchenko, who was seated in the car's parlor, jolted and spilled his vodka. He was angrily dabbing at his trousers when Stacy entered.

"And?" asked Korchenko, with no preamble whatsoever.

"He is on the job," Stacy replied.

"Good." Satisfied that his pants were as clean as they were going to get, Korchenko set aside the moist handkerchief.

"I ordered lunch," said Stacy, removing his gloves. "Brook trout with almonds, braised carrots, rice pilaf, a nice Chablis, and chocolate mousse for dessert."

Korchenko nodded curtly, then asked, "Where did he go, this Skye Fargo?"

"He found a cab driver who had apparently seen Francesca yesterday," Stacy said. "The two of them took off in something of a rush." He bent to look out through one of the car's side windows. "I hate these layovers. It's so difficult to find decent restaurants that will deliver."

"All you think of is food, Franklin," Korchenko said, staring at his soiled handkerchief.

Wearily, Stacy straightened. "Were that it were so, Vladimir. Were that it were so."

By two in the afternoon, Francesca had convinced Mae that she really had to do something about the parlor. Besides, there was nothing else to do in this town. Everything was so . . . provincial.

But there were shops, by God, shops right across the street, and shops needed to be investigated.

"Don't go gettin' your tail feathers in a twist," Mae said, working at the tiny buttons on her gloves. "I'm coming!"

"You could have fooled me," said Francesca, smiling. She'd been ready for over an hour.

They stepped outside into the overcast day. No rain yet, but the sky was heavy with cloudy promises.

"Where first?" Mae asked. At least, Francesca thought, she was beginning to look a bit excited about the prospect of redecorating.

"Let's go to the end of the block and work our way back, shall we?" Francesca said brightly.

She felt free for the first time in ages. She felt no presences, evil or otherwise, loitering about her. She certainly didn't feel Korchenko or Stacy anywhere near. Not like on the ship, nor when she had landed in New York. Not even like St. Louis. In St. Louis, a woman in the next room had been murdered.

Accidentally, of course.

Well, the victim had been tallish and redheaded.

How could that lout, Stacy, have known in the dark that it wasn't Francesca?

"Pig," she muttered.

"What, dear?" asked Mae.

Francesca smiled. "Nothing, Mae, nothing at all."

Skye Fargo held his position until the two women had passed him, until they got a good half-block down the way and turned into a shop. Notions, that was what it said in the window. He didn't know what the hell "notions" were, never having stepped inside a notions shop. And he didn't intend to start now.

So he didn't go in. Just folded his paper up under his arm, moseyed down the way so that he could keep an eye on the front door, then leaned back and pretended to read again.

Half an hour later, they emerged, and the short dark one was carrying a few packages. She was a looker, but she paled in comparison to Francesca Ponti.

Fargo was certain that he'd never seen such a striking woman in all his days, and he'd seen quite a few. Between her lush leggy figure with its tiny waist and full bust, that gorgeous red hair, and those limpid emerald eyes, a man could get lost real quick if he didn't keep his wits about him.

And just sitting out here, spying on them, Fargo was about to lose his.

"Not on your tintype, Fargo," he growled at himself as he watched them enter the next shop. "Just keep your britches on and your brain in gear till you do the job, boyo."

The admonition didn't do anything to discourage the erection he felt straining against his store-bought trousers, though.

Two hours later he had finished reading the newspaper, front to back, and decided it was time that he followed them inside the shop where they were dallying now, if only to buy himself something else to read.

But when he stepped through the doorway, he ran smack into Francesca Ponti.

Her packages fell and scattered all over the floor and she let out a small, surprised, *"Oof!"* Then she added an "Oh, my!" when she belatedly saw Fargo.

Fargo recovered immediately, and started picking up her packages. "Terribly clumsy of me, madam," he said as he handed them to her, then stooped for more. "Can't tell you how sorry I am."

"Well, I should say so!" huffed Mae, who wasn't far behind.

"Nonsense, darling," Francesca said to Mae. "It was a surprise to both of us." She took the last package from Fargo. "Thank you, Mister . . . ?"

"Fargo, ma'am," he said without thinking, and doffed his hat. And then he added, rather lamely, "Fargo P. Langtree. From Wichita. At your service, ladies." He nodded to Mae, while he was at it, and mentally kicked himself for letting his name slip, even if he had covered it. He hoped.

Francesca had more of an effect on him than he wanted to admit.

And then, although it was somewhat belatedly, he had a sterling idea.

"May I?" he asked as he took back Francesca's packages. "A lovely lady like you shouldn't have to be toting such a load."

Francesca smiled, although Mae, who stood behind with her arms piled high, glowered slightly.

"How kind of you, Mr. Langtree," Francesca said, her green eyes full of promises, whether she meant them or not.

Likely not, thought Fargo, *but a man can dream, can't he?*

"I am Miss Francesca Ponti, and this is my friend, Mrs. Mae Purvis."

Fargo tipped his hat again and reached for some of Mae's packages. "May I?" he asked, filling his arms. "Pleased to meet you, ladies. Now, whereabouts were you headed?"

Six o'clock found Fargo nervously pacing in the lobby of the Washington Arms. It was actually a pretty fair lobby in which to pace. Broad, long, and high-ceilinged, its carpets were thick and its chairs comfortable.

But he was wearing a path in the carpet.

Normally, he wouldn't have been in such a tizzy. Normally, a thing like this wouldn't have flustered him in the slightest. He was, after all, a man of the world—the world west of the Mississippi, at least. He'd met up with all kinds of people from murderers to governors, from timid, mousy women to loud, brassy whores to those pushy women's-rights types. He'd seen just about everything.

But he'd never seen anything like Francesca Ponti.

He'd asked them to dine with him, the two of them, seeing as how he couldn't figure out how to break up the set. They hadn't said a word about Mae's house being a house of ill-repute when he'd dropped them at their door, and neither had he. Francesca had simply taken her packages, thanked him, and said good-bye. Of course, there had been paragraphs unspoken in that, "Good-bye, Mr. Langtree."

Now that he'd been apart from her for a few hours and had had time to mull over just what those unspoken paragraphs might be, he was at as much of a loss as he ever had been.

And then he saw her.

She was resplendent in a cranberry-colored gown that was out of place in Lincoln but just right for her. How on earth she had made it up the street without half the male population following her was beyond Fargo. As it was, every head in the place turned to stare when she walked in.

She seemed oblivious to it, though, Fargo noticed as he went to meet her. She only had eyes for him.

And she was alone. No sign of Mae Purvis.

Good.

"Good evening, Miss Ponti," he said, and was conscious that he was beaming more than he ought. After all, this was business, he reminded himself. She had stolen something and he was bound to take it back.

But he forgot all about that when she turned that smile on him—her teeth were perfect pearls—and said, "I do hope you don't mind, but Mrs. Purvis sends her apologies, Mr. Langtree."

"No problem," Fargo said, and held out his arm. "No problem at all. I've asked the restaurant to hold a table for us. Shall we?"

"Certainly, Mr. Langtree," she said. She took his arm, and they proceeded into the restaurant.

5

What was he up to?

The true identity of this Mr. Langtree had dawned on Francesca roughly thirty minutes after she'd made his acquaintance. She hadn't recognized him right off the bat only because he wasn't dressed in his usual attire, and because it hadn't occurred to her to look for him this far north.

In fact, it hadn't occurred to her to look for him at all.

If she'd seen him on that famous paint horse of his, and clad in his usual bucks, she would have run the other way.

But she hadn't, and had thus gotten some time to know him, and when she and Mae had been escorted over their threshold—and she'd given her promise to meet him for supper—the realization had suddenly settled over her like a veil. With a little help from Mae, who had said, "What was his first name again?"

"Fargo, I think," she'd said as she watched him walk up the street, back to his hotel. And then she'd said, "Fargo!" again and smacked herself in the head. "Of course! I am truly an idiot."

"What's that, dear?" Mae had asked, hanging up her shawl.

"Nothing," Francesca had replied. "Nothing at all."

But she went directly to her room and just sat there for a good long time.

For heaven's sake, who wouldn't recognize the famous Skye Fargo? His picture had appeared in any number of papers over the past years. She'd even read a book about him—one of those cheap, dime novel things—on the train from New York.

Acclaimed a hero and a saint by some, and a rough scoundrel by others, he was a famous man regardless of which opinion you believed.

So what on earth was he doing in Lincoln, going under an assumed name, and escorting two ladies of questionable repute to their door?

It had to be the jewels.

Except that nobody except Vladimir and Franklin knew she had them.

Could he be in their employ?

She had puzzled over this for the rest of the afternoon, changing her mind as often as the girls traipsing up and down the stairs outside her room changed clients. And when suppertime came, she was still undecided.

If I were wise, she had thought as she changed clothes and prepared to meet Fargo at the Washington Arms, *I would go straight past the hotel, march on to the depot, and get on the next train going anywhere.*

But then, she wasn't always wise, at least in matters of the heart. And she found Fargo interesting. Handsome, certainly. The rumors of his scandalous prowess in the bedroom were nearly as abundant—and legendary—as the stories of his courage.

And so she found herself seated, that evening, at a small table in the Washington's grand dining room, ordering an appetizer of fresh oysters shipped in on ice, direct from Nantucket.

"Oysters, eh?" Fargo, alias Langtree, said. He looked at the waiter. "I'll have those as well. The lady and I will have two nice steaks. Mine rare. And your's?" he asked Francesca.

"Medium," she said.

"With potatoes au gratin and garden peas," Fargo continued, his eyes on the menu, "and a bottle of your best wine. We'll order dessert later. Is that all right with you, Miss Ponti?" He smiled at her over the menu's rim. He did have the dreamiest eyes . . .

Dreamy? My Lord, she hadn't thought of a man's eyes that way since she was a schoolgirl! What was wrong with her?

But she said, "Lovely, Mr. Langtree."

The waiter bowed and slipped away.

"What brings you to Lincoln, Miss Ponti?" he asked. Those clear blue eyes of his cut into her like knives made of honed ice. "You surely out-class this town," he went on.

She felt herself color hotly, but said, "Thank you, I'm sure, but you flatter me. And I'm en route to San Francisco, Mr. Langtree. My home is there. And as I told you this afternoon, Mrs. Purvis is a longtime friend of mine."

Fargo couldn't know how long, Francesca thought. She and Mae had met in a home for orphaned girls in New York when they were both twelve, and had been fast friends ever since. In fact, they often laughed about the "fast" part. Mae's parents had died of smallpox. Francesca's only surviving parent, her Italian immigrant father, had been killed in a street accident. She'd lost her mother shortly after she was born.

"I thought it well to pay Mae a long overdue call, so long as I was journeying across country," she finished. "She is a darling."

"Ah, yes," he said thoughtfully. "Mrs. Purvis seemed terribly nice. Did you tell me you were coming from New York?"

"By way of the continent," she replied. Was it the jewels he was after? Perhaps some other business, some old mark finally catching up with her. If only he'd give her a hint! "And you, Mr. Langtree?"

"Oh, I'm just passing through myself," he said. She could find no ulterior motive in his eyes. But then, she was nearly drowning in them.

"On your way to where?" she asked. Small talk was too quickly becoming her only life preserver.

"Oddly enough, I'm bound for San Francisco, too," he said with an absolutely charming grin. She wanted to run her fingers through that beard of his. No, she wanted to tiptoe through it, barefoot.

"How nice," she said. "I wonder if we will be taking the same train."

"Very possibly," he said, and he didn't wink, she was sure he hadn't, but why did she think that he had? She flushed despite herself.

"That would be very nice," she replied.

"Ah!" he said, twisting slightly in his chair toward the approaching waiter. "Our oysters are here."

It was the damnedest thing, Fargo thought. All during dinner she'd been a perfect lady. Hadn't said or even implied anything even slightly out of the ordinary. But he had the oddest—and strongest—feeling that she wanted him in the worst way.

Nearly as much as he wanted her.

Maybe this was the way that rich, fancy people seduced each other, by asking for the salt to be passed or commenting on the consistency of the lemon ice. If so, she was seducing him just as surely as he was seducing her. And neither one of them had said or done anything that was the least bit sexual.

But you still could have cut the air with a butter knife.

"Have you a wife, Mr. Langtree? I fear she must miss you terribly when you take these long trips."

"No, no wife, Miss Ponti," he'd replied with a shrug.

"The pepper, please, Mr. Langtree?"

"Certainly, Miss Ponti."

Hell, he'd almost forgotten why he was here in the first place. Not quite, though.

"I find the constantly changing scenery as I pass through the countryside most refreshing, don't you?" she asked.

"Yes, indeed. Would you care for more wine?"

If she had that tiara, it wasn't on her. It was likely

back at Mae Purvis's place, salted away. She wouldn't have taken a chance on shipping it ahead. There were too many opportunities for it to be inadvertently lost or stolen. No, she had to have it close.

But not too close.

The bill paid and the last dish cleared, their last cups of coffee downed, they rose from their table.

Now, how in the blue blazes, Fargo wondered, *do I ask the all-important, oak-toppling question when all through dinner we've just been picking windfall acorns off the ground? And damned politely, too.*

"My dear Miss Ponti," he began, when they entered the lobby, "I was wondering. That is, would you care to, um . . . ?"

Quite warmly, she took his arm and gazed into his eyes. "Why, I'd be delighted to see your room, Mr. Langtree."

Well, it wasn't exactly what he'd wanted. He'd wanted to be invited back to her place, where he might have some chance to go through her things once she was asleep.

But still . . . *Eureka!*

He tipped his head in a slight bow.

"This way, Miss Ponti," he said with a grin, and led her up the staircase.

She was something, all right.

Once he'd closed and locked the door behind them, she said, "They've given you quite a charming room, Mr. Langtree," and then turned and stepped into his arms.

It was like holding a dream.

His clothes, then hers, fell off as if by magic, and she was even more glorious naked than he could have imagined. Those lean, long, endless legs, that tiny waist, those full lush breasts . . .

Not a freckle, not the tiniest scar or birthmark marred her.

In other words, she was perfect. Her red hair fell

down over her shoulders in a loose, wavy mass of soft russet curls, making an impossibly beautiful frame for those large, long-lashed green eyes.

Her mouth was impossibly soft, her eager lips ripe, and her throat long, white, and swan-like. She wrapped her arms about his neck again and kissed him deeply, softly, warmly, her slim hands traveling lightly up and down the hard muscles of his back and coming to rest on his backside.

If this was the way that those anonymous crowned heads of Europe made love, he was all for being a crowned head. Or making love to one of their consorts. And if she had indeed stolen those jewels, she'd earned every single one of them.

He picked her up in his arms and carried her to the bed, nuzzling her breasts as he went.

"Why, Mr. Langtree," she whispered with a smile. "How very forward of you."

"Call me Fargo, Miss Ponti," he said as he gently put her down upon the sheets, then hovered over her.

"Call me Francesca," she breathed.

He kissed her, at the same time gently running a hand down the length of her body, skimming her flawless flesh. Downward his fingers crept, down over the slight bell of ribs, down over the narrow waist. Down around the curve of her hip, then up onto the softness of her belly. Then lower, to the soft, triangular pelt of fiery hair at the juncture of her thighs.

He brushed it with his palm first, then eased his fingers deeper, first touching skin, then deeper, inside. She was wet and hot and more than ready for him, and she let out a tiny, mewling sound against his lips when he touched her.

Her legs eased apart, and her hand swept over his back, urging him to investigate further.

He abandoned her lips, then, and began kissing his way down her body, following the path his hand had taken. By the time he got to her inner thighs, she was pushing herself against him almost frantically.

And so he took her.

She fit him like a glove, and she matched him thrust for thrust. With her feet tucked back for purchase and her thighs gripping his hips as if she'd never let him go, she pushed herself up off the mattress, tilting her pelvis at an exquisite angle.

Faster and faster Fargo pumped, losing himself, losing everything in the incandescent glory that was Francesca. One of her hands raked his shoulders, urging him on; the other twisted the bedclothes. Her eyes were closed, her head arched back, her panting, gasping mouth open as her head whipped back and forth in the thralls of passion.

Fargo pummeled her harder. She seemed to require it of him, to always ask for more, though neither of them could speak, let alone think.

And just when he was certain that he was going to explode, explode like he never had before and maybe disappoint her, possibly let her down, she convulsed beneath him, shuddered wildly, and let out a soft, keening cry.

And this toppled him over the edge as well. The tickle in his loins that had grown into a bonfire suddenly burst into a full-scale conflagration, and he felt himself gratefully emptying into her, all in a sweet, sweet rush.

They lay there, shaking and panting for quite some time.

At last, she spoke.

"Fargo, darling?"

"Yes, my love?" he said, his fingers stroking a wisp of damp hair from her temple.

She smiled just a little, cocked her head, and said, "Exactly what train do you plan to take West? I want to be on it."

Franklin Stacy tiredly climbed the Pullman's steps and let himself in the back door. A light at the other end of the short hall told him that Vladimir was still up. Wanting details, no doubt.

"Ah, Franklin," Korchenko said when Stacy emerged from the hallway and into the glow of lamps.

Korchenko was taking a late supper. Meats and cheeses were set out on platters on either side of little dishes of pickles and such, and a loaf of fresh bread. An open bottle of merlot sat breathing on the sideboard. Stacy licked his lips without realizing it.

He took a step toward the buffet, but Korchenko stopped him. "Report, first, Franklin," he said gently, but in a tone that indicated he meant business. Stacy reminded himself that you didn't cross Vladimir Korchenko. Not if you wished to live another day.

He retraced his steps and sat down in a chair. Running his fingers over the red velvet, he said, "There is really nothing to report. She went to his hotel. They had dinner. And then they went upstairs."

Korchenko lifted a brow. "And then? Did you follow her home?"

"I had no wish to stand on the street the whole night, Vladimir," Stacy said, attempting to cloak his impatience.

"The whole night?" asked Korchenko.

Stacy nodded. As patiently as he could, he said, "His rooms are on the second floor. The end windows. I believe I have already conveyed this information to you, have I not, Vladimir?"

"Yes, my dear Franklin, you have," said Korchenko. "And it would be well for you to remember to whom you are speaking."

Something about the tone in which these words were spoken sent a little frisson up Stacy's spine, and he stiffened.

"It was not my wish to offend you," he said. "My apologies if I have done so."

Korchenko was silent for a little too long, but then he looked away, and said, "Very well. Go on, Franklin, my dear."

Stacy realized he'd been squeezing the chair's arm, and let go of it, surreptitiously stroking the velvet pile back into place.

"They went upstairs," he said. "The lights in his room were turned up, and then went out. I waited a

44

goodly amount of time, but the lady in question did not show her face again."

"She did not leave by the rear entrance?"

"No. I had the boy stationed there."

"Had?"

Stacy took a breath, then nodded. "Yes, Vladimir. I left him watching the windows. If anything happens, he will follow."

Korchenko lifted his smouldering cigar from the ashtray with a white and bony hand. "This is a good boy? Trustworthy?"

"Yes, Vladimir."

"And when he has served his purpose?"

"An urchin. No one will miss him."

Korchenko nodded this time. It was a curt nod, such as one would give after reviewing the troops, Stacy thought.

Korchenko took a thoughtful puff on his cigar. "Most interesting, Franklin. Fargo and the woman, I mean. I would not have expected her to bed him so soon. Or he her, for that matter. How do you read the situation?"

Stacy shrugged. He was having to force himself not to look at the bounty spread out on the sideboard. He could smell the meats. The pickles tickled and teased at his nostrils. The merlot beckoned from afar.

He said, "It is not for me to say, Vladimir."

Korchenko studied him for a moment through a haze of cigar smoke, and then said, "You are learning, Franklin. Very well. Eat something."

6

Francesca woke before the dawn, and Fargo woke with her. They made love again, slowly, leisurely, with less of last night's urgency, this time with more care, and more caring.

And when they had finished, when the last kiss had been spent and the last whisper breathed, she took her leave.

Fargo watched her from his windows, watched her emerge from the building and make her way up the street in the thin gray light of early morning.

It took him a moment to see the boy.

On the opposite side of the street, the kid—scrawny, unkempt, about ten years old, and dressed in rags—followed Francesca at a distance.

He did it fairly well, Fargo thought. He wasn't obvious about it. He stopped and tarried here and there, usually to peer into a garbage bin or pick up something at the curb and study it. He was a ragamuffin, the type to sort through trash and grub out an old potato or a crust of bread.

The boy followed Francesca to her door—which Fargo learned by finally opening the window and canting himself out—then tarried for a while before he took off at a lope that turned into a run.

Running to where? Fargo wondered.

And running to whom?

Quickly, Fargo dressed and raced down the stairs. If he could follow the boy before too many people were up and about and completely obliterated his footprints, he might find out where the kid was headed.

Still fumbling with his jacket, Fargo raced out the hotel's double front doors and down toward Mae Purvis's house, where a number of saddle horses drowsed at the rail, awaiting their tardy masters.

He crossed the street, picked up the boy's small footprints, fresh in the frosty dew, and began to follow them at a trot.

They wound him through town, through back alleys and, at one point, up a drainpipe and over three rooftops. By the time Fargo climbed down from the last, he was panting and cursing. It was mixed with a healthy degree of admiration, though. The kid knew this town like the palm of his hand.

But when he came to a large crossroads, already beginning to bustle with short-tempered morning traffic, he lost the track. He circled around a few times, but by then the sun was up. Bustling pedestrians hurried and shoved past on the sidewalks, churning any sign of prints underfoot. The dew had evaporated into the chilled morning air, anyway.

Shaking his head, he gave up and started back toward the Washington.

And as he walked, he thought about Francesca.

Oh, she was certainly something, wasn't she? He'd never imagined that any woman would be so tender and regal and sensuous and mannered—and wildly mannerless—all at the same time. She was incredible. He was half in love with her already.

"Get over it, Fargo," he muttered to himself. "She's a thief and a cheat for starters. And all that aside, she's way out of your class."

Miles out of it, he thought.

But then, why had she come up to his room in the first place?

The thought hadn't occurred to him before, and he berated himself for it. Why, indeed, had she made love to a total stranger, a stranger she'd just met that afternoon in the provinces—in Lincoln, Nebraska, for

God's sake—when she had been a paramour to royalty? A king, for all he knew.

Was she slumming?

He would have said yes, but her manner, her fervor, and the way she'd made love to him, didn't indicate that "slumming" was exactly the word he was looking for.

And while Mae Purvis's home was obviously—to his practiced eye, anyhow—a cat house, Francesca hadn't been plying that trade. At least, she'd asked him for no money. It wasn't even discussed.

Why, then?

Could she know something was up?

And if so, what?

And who was that kid? The boy had been watching her rather than Fargo, there was no doubt about it. He'd probably been standing out there all night in the cold, slapping his shoulders, rubbing his hands together, stomping his feet, and staring up at Fargo's windows, just waiting for some hint of light and life.

Just the thought of it—some freezing kid timing them with a stopwatch—gave him the collywobbles.

Somebody had to have hired the boy, Fargo was pretty sure, but he was at a loss as to who the lad's employer might be. Stacy was back in Kansas City, so it couldn't have been him. And besides, he'd have no reason for it. He'd already hired Fargo.

Could somebody else possibly be after this damned tiara? The Pinkertons? Another agent of this anonymous government head that Stacy claimed to represent? Maybe an unknown third party, out to steal the tiara all over again, this time from Francesca Ponti.

Well, he'd have a few hours to think over those plaguing questions. Francesca was meeting him for lunch at the Washington, and then they had planned to spend a long, leisurely afternoon together. It would be in his rooms, although neither of them had said as much. But it was understood.

His problem was how to move the festivities from the Washington down to Mae Purvis's house, to Francesca's room, where he could get a look at her luggage, and hopefully have the time to go through it.

Barring that, he'd have to figure out some way to get her to confide in him.

But if she knew something, if she had the slightest clue that anything was amiss, he wouldn't get a chance at either option.

Damn!

At last, he reached his hotel and slowly trudged up the wide carpeted steps to his rooms. It was going to be a long day.

Francesca showed up at noon on the dot.

Today she was dressed all in a lush shade of pink that brought out the roses in her cheeks and made her eyes look even greener, if that was possible.

Fargo's first inclination was to skip lunch and just take her upstairs, but he kept on telling himself: *Five thousand dollars, five thousand dollars . . .*

He talked her into taking the noon meal elsewhere, if for no other reason than to make his room less convenient, less beckoning.

"The Charleston Café," he said, ushering her out the hotel doors. "It comes highly recommended, and as luck would have it, it's just around the corner."

"How charming," she said with a smile that simply dazzled him.

Arm in arm, they walked the short distance to the café, and as they did, Fargo kept an eye out. Sure enough, there was that boy again, slipping and sliding through the shadows across the way like a puma on the hunt. Who the hell was he?

Fargo was beginning to obsess on the subject.

As he and Francesca ate their lunch—actually a very fine repast that included truffled chicken breasts in a light burgundy sauce, buttered and parsleyed potatoes cut in the shapes of little roses, and a salad of artichoke hearts—he slowly maneuvered the conversation toward her lodgings. He was trying to figure out how in the world to broach the subject of Mrs. Mae

Purvis being, well, a lady of the evening, and trying to figure out how to make that sound like a good thing.

But he never got the chance.

She kept switching the subject every time he thought he was close. She switched it to horse racing, then European trains, then the current political intrigues in the English court, and on and on. And the trouble was that she was so good at it, knew her subjects so well and was so goddamned interesting, that he always fell into it and only realized too late that he'd gotten completely off the track.

Damn her anyway!

Well, maybe not. She was too beautiful, too sweet, too appealing for any man to curse. But she was clever all right. Very clever. And, Fargo realized with a start, she was onto him. Why else all the far-flung topics of conversation?

So he finally gave up and just played along. There was more than one way to skin a cat.

After he paid what turned out to be a staggering bill—he was beginning to think that Stacy wasn't paying him enough—they walked back around the corner.

"Let's go to your place," he said, giving it one last try. It wasn't an elegant attempt, but it might get the job done.

But she squeezed his arm, looked up with those cool green eyes, impossibly full of fire, and replied, "My goodness, Fargo, I don't believe that would set too well with dear Mae."

Shot down again.

He wasn't above taking the afternoon with her anyway. Hell, maybe she'd blurt something out in the throes of passion. Maybe he could slip her a sleeping powder and scoot down the street to Mae's and have a surreptitious look at her room.

Maybe not.

And that damned kid was still following them! From the corner of his eye, Fargo caught a glimpse of him, rags and all, ducking into the mouth of an alley.

"Very well, darling," he said with a smile that

wasn't entirely sincere. He turned her toward the Washington's front doors. "Shall we?"

"I thought you'd never ask," she purred.

Fargo dined alone that night.

After a long afternoon of lovemaking, during which she'd neither blurted out anything in the throes of passion nor confessed anything in her sleep, she'd gone back to Mae's. She'd said that she really must spend some time with her poor, neglected hostess, wish as she might to stay with him.

Fargo had been gracious.

He'd said, "Of course I understand, Francesca." And then he'd lifted her voluminous skirts, which she'd just put back on, and taken her once more time, against the wall.

"You have the most interesting way of saying goodbye, Fargo Langtree," she'd said a good half-hour later, a mischievous twinkle in her eyes.

He'd winked at her. "It's a gift," he'd said, and gave her breast a last caress.

And after she'd left, he'd watched out the window. Again, the small boy—he was tow-headed, Fargo could see that now—had appeared from the shadows and dogged her down the street, melding into the alley across the way once she went inside.

At least the kid wasn't following him. That was a plus, anyway.

After he ate, he went back up to his rooms and changed clothes, back into his buckskins. They felt mighty good after that scratchy collar. The only thing that would have felt better—aside from Francesca, that was—would have been the Ovaro between his knees.

He wondered how the horse was doing. He'd left him at a good stable, the best in Kansas City, and he'd paid for extra grain and exercise and a thorough, once-a-day currying and brushing. They'd better be taking good care of his Ovaro—or else.

But then, Rose would see to it. She was awfully

fond of the horse, too, he thought with a grin. The Ovaro would probably find himself with an abundance of daily carrots and lump sugar.

And if nothing else, Rose was awfully fond of the money Fargo was going to have when he found that damned crown, too.

He waited until it was good and dark, and then he slipped out the hotel's back door and made his way down the alley, between piles of junk and piles of other things he'd rather not think about.

A couple of dogs barked at him and there was a cat fight in progress a couple of blocks away, but other than that, nothing was out of the ordinary. Mae Purvis's house wasn't far at all, no more than a block.

He knew the place before he got to it.

There had been several saddle horses tethered out front this morning, but the back alley was where the monied trade stashed their rigs. Even at this early hour, there were three tied along the fence out back: an elegant brougham and two pretty-nice slicked-up buggies, one of them with silver fittings.

The gentlemen in question must have driven themselves to Mae Purvis's, for there were no drivers waiting with the horses.

He patted one of the dozing hackneys hitched to the brougham as he passed, and eased himself up over the back fence.

He came down on the other side, light as a feather. No one was in the yard, but light, music, and laughter leaked out the windows. Everybody had a good time at Mae's, it would seem.

After he found a hiding place and was nestled in the thick bushy hedge with his back to the fence, he settled in to watch the upstairs windows.

He didn't have long to wait. About a half hour after he'd hunkered down to watch the girls' lights turn up and down, up and down, and a procession of men pass through their rooms, a light came on in a previously gloomy chamber on the third floor.

He watched Francesca pass the window and go to

the mirror to check her hair. She leaned down, fiddling with something out of his line of vision, and then she moved again. The lights went out once more.

He waited, though. And pretty soon, he caught a glimpse of her, downstairs, going into a small side parlor with Mae, then closing the pocket doors behind them.

Now was his chance.

Fargo crept up to the house, ducking beneath the windows and keeping his footfalls light, until he made his way to the drainpipe. He tugged on the drainpipe to test it.

It felt solid enough, and he pulled himself aloft, swung his legs up, and heaved himself to the first floor's roof.

He worked his way carefully along the top of the overhang, over the shingles, and up to the next level toward the window of Francesca's room, which was still dark.

When he reached it, he found that she'd left it cracked a couple of inches. Thank God for fresh air lovers, that was all he had to say. She'd just saved him a bit of work, and possibly some breakage that would have betrayed him.

He eased the window up. It creaked at the effort, but the noise downstairs was too loud for anyone to have heard it. He slipped inside.

It took a moment for his eyes to become accustomed to the lack of light inside, but gradually the room took shadowy form. He made out the trunks almost immediately, and knelt beside them.

Twenty minutes later, he had gone through each one, searching the tops and bottoms for false drawers, the sides for split panels, and found nothing. Absolutely nothing, aside from ball gowns that she'd have no reason to wear in anywhere as backwater and gauche as Lincoln, Nebraska.

Her hand luggage?

Next he moved to this. There was a soft-sided suitcase, a nightcase, and two hatboxes, but he found she'd unpacked most of the contents. After searching what was left in them, he went through her drawers, then her chifforobe.

Nothing.

What in the hell had she done with the Moldavian Crown?

Maybe he'd missed something. He was about to start all over, this time emptying the trunks and going through them from top to bottom, from latch to liner, when he heard something in the hall.

Of course, he'd heard feet clicking—and boots clomping—past all evening, but these footsteps stopped. He had slithered out the window and was out on the roof holding his breath, when the door opened.

The light came up. It had to be Francesca, although he didn't dare risk a peek. He eased away, and by the time she came to the window and placed a questioning hand on the pane, he was already on the ground and secreted by a bush.

He watched as she studied the pane.

Did she scowl?

He couldn't tell.

She shook her pretty head, and then pushed the window down to its previous position. Her mouth moved, but he couldn't make out the words. All he could see was that she was beautiful.

And then she closed the curtains.

7

Fargo was about to stand up when he heard the snap of a twig behind him, no more than two feet away.

Without thinking, he whirled, his gun drawn.

"D-d-don't shoot, Mister!" peeped a small voice. He couldn't tell if it was a child or a woman. It sure wasn't a man.

Fargo squinted into the bushes, but it was too black in there to see a damned thing.

He wiggled the nose of his gun. "Come out," he said. "Slow."

Timidly, a small, terrified face emerged from the shrubs. The blond head and ragtag clothing identified the boy immediately.

Fargo sighed and holstered his gun. "You're the kid that's been tailing Francesca," he whispered. "What's your name, boy?"

"Don't know any Francesca," the boy said in a quavering voice. "And I gotta go. My ma will, um, be fixin' supper."

"Sure she will," Fargo said. He slid a look over his shoulder, at the house. People laughed, sang, climbed the stairs, drank another brandy, smoked another cigar. They hadn't been spotted yet.

"I asked you, son, what your name was," he said again.

The boy bolted, but Fargo caught the fabric at his shoulder.

A split second later it tore with a sick ripping sound,

and Fargo had to run a few steps before he caught the boy again.

He glanced quickly back at Mae Purvis's bright windows, then pulled the boy, thrashing, into the depths of the bushes.

"Cut it out, kid!" he hissed. He pushed away the twig that was stabbing him in the face. "Just calm the hell down. I'm not gonna hurt you."

"Says you," the boy answered, with questionable confidence. He stood there, stiff as a board in his torn shirt and his rags.

Christ, he must be freezing to death, Fargo thought with a shake of his head.

"How'd you get in here?" he asked, nodding his head toward the fence that ran around the back of the Purvis house. It was a six-foot fence. There was no way that a boy of nine or ten could have climbed it.

"The gate," answered the boy.

Fargo rolled his eyes. Now, why hadn't he thought of that? He took a good, firm hold on the boy's collar. "Lead the way," he said.

The boy made another break for it once they were free of the hedge, and yet another after they made it out into the alley, but Fargo was ready for him both times. On the last attempt, he simply lifted the lad up off the ground by his collar and let him kick his legs in the air for a minute.

"You gonna be nice?" he asked after he set the boy on his feet again.

"Maybe," the boy said sullenly.

They started walking back up the alley, toward the Washington. "You going to tell me your name?" Fargo asked again.

"Bobby," the boy answered sullenly, without looking at him.

"That the whole thing?"

"Bobby Farrell. And what's it to you, anyhow, Mister?"

Fargo hadn't let go of Bobby's collar yet, not by a

long shot. "My name's Fargo, Bobby Farrell. Pleased to meet you. I think."

"Feeling ain't mutual," the boy said with a scowl. His hair didn't look to have been washed in weeks. Months, maybe.

"You out on your own, Bobby?" Fargo asked kindly.

Suddenly, the boy wheeled toward him, and Fargo nearly lost his grip.

"I ain't goin' back to that orphanage, Mister, I'll tell you that right now," the boy announced fiercly. A dog started barking in one of the yards. "If'n you take me back, I'll just scoot away again. And I'll keep on runnin' till I get clean shed of you, even if I have to go all the way to Hong Kong or London or even France in Europe! And shut up, dog!"

The dog stopped barking and Fargo blinked. He liked the kid's spark. "That's quite an outburst, there, Bobby. I take it you mean to make a clean escape?"

The boy straightened a bit and nodded. He eyed Fargo up and down, apparently for the first time. "Hey, you ain't dressed like one of them trustees," he said suspiciously. "You know, one of them orphan-catcher people. They usually wear black suits."

"That's because I'm not," Fargo replied.

"What'd you say your name was?"

"Fargo."

The boy's eyes slowly grew from scared and angry slits to round and white-ringed saucers. "Dressed in bucks? You're not, I mean, are you Skye Fargo? I mean the real Skye Fargo? The one they call the Trailsman?" Quickly, he looked up and down the dark alley. "Where's the Ovaro?"

Fargo just stared at him. Finally, he sighed and asked, "Does everybody read those stupid books?"

"Hot damn!" said Bobby, suddenly all excitement. "You need a sidekick, Fargo? I can ride, sort of, and I can—"

"Whoa up there!" said Fargo, letting go of the kid's

shirt. This boy wasn't going anywhere; not now. In fact, he had a feeling that he'd have to scrape him off with a spatula to get rid of him.

"Well, I'm not in the market for a sidekick right at the minute," he said thoughtfully, "but you can sure help me out."

"Anything," the boy breathed, and Fargo found himself thinking that maybe those dime novels weren't all bad. At least, they'd slowed down this kid long enough to get him to listen.

"First off, I'm feelin' kind of peckish," Fargo lied, giving a rub to his stomach. The poor kid didn't look like he'd had anything decent to eat in a coon's age. "What do you say we go back to the hotel and get us some grub? You know, eat first, parley later."

Bobby said, "Well, um . . ." and dug his toe in the dirt.

Fargo quickly added, "It's on me, Bobby. I'm gonna ply you for information." He grinned.

Suddenly the boy was all sunshine and smiles, even if they were covered by four layers of grime. "Okay," he said. "You bet!"

Fargo snuck him in through the hotel's back door, secreted him into his room, then went back downstairs and ordered up some food and a hot bath. The bellmen with the water almost beat him back upstairs.

They trooped in, pouring bucket after steaming bucket into the tub, while Bobby waited patiently and silently in the chifforobe where Fargo had tucked him away. At one point, he sneezed quite loudly and a bellman looked over his shoulder, but Fargo wiped at his nose and said, "Getting chilly out there."

The bellman shrugged and emptied his buckets.

The food arrived on the heels of the last bellman, and at last Fargo opened the chifforobe door. Bobby burst out and headed straight for the silver-covered dish on the sideboard.

But Fargo caught his shirt again and said, "Wash first, eat later. And wash good. I'm gonna check your ears."

"But—" Bobby started.

"No buts," Fargo said firmly. He was likely going to have to fumigate the chifforobe as it was. In the light, the kid was ten times grubbier than he'd looked outside, if that were possible.

But Bobby looked so crestfallen—and so damned hungry—that Fargo weakened. He lifted one of the shiny silver plate covers and pulled out half a roast beef sandwich.

"Here," he said, offering it to the boy, who greedily snatched it from him. He had already downed half of it before Fargo said, "To hold you over."

"You're him, ain't you?" Bobby asked around a mouthful of sandwich. "I mean, you're the dude she's been steppin' out with. I didn't know you at first. You're dressed so different."

"I am, indeed, that dude," said Fargo gravely. "And don't try to grab the other half of that sandwich," he added when Bobby's hand snaked toward the covered dish. "Go get cleaned up."

"Aw, jeez!"

"No arguments."

While the boy bathed, Fargo went through his bag and pulled out his spare set of bucks. They'd be awful damned big on the kid, but those clothes he'd been wearing were practically crawling across the floor.

He cracked the bathroom door. To the sound of splashing, he tossed in the bucks, saying, "Put these on when you're finished. Just roll up the cuffs and sleeves."

He dropped the kid's old clothes in the trash.

But then he thought that young Mr. Bobby Farrell might have something in the pockets that he might not necessarily want to go to the rag pickers. He pulled over the waste basket and, gingerly, began to search through the boy's pockets.

He found the usual small boy items, although they were in poorer condition than most: a rusted pocket-knife, a small ball of string, worn ticket stub for the local marionette theater, what appeared to be a dried toad, a tin whistle, four grimy pennies (one flattened on a railroad track), and part of a wizened orange, carefully wrapped in a dirty handkerchief.

For some reason, the orange got Fargo to feeling real bad for the kid. He stared at it for a while, then tossed it away. This was one kid that wouldn't be picking his dinner out of the trash anymore. Not if Fargo had anything to do with it.

And he also found something very curious. It was a small silver coin, bearing the profile of a man unfamiliar to him, and inscribed in a foreign language.

He recognized one word of it, though.

Moldavia.

"*Hmmmm,*" he said, and thoughtfully leaned back, flipping the coin over and over in his hand.

Someone had been in her room, there was no doubt of it.

After she closed the curtains, the first thing Francesca did was check her trunk. Frantically, she found the ballgown and felt for the crown in the folds of the bustle.

It was still there, thank God, but she eased the seam apart anyway. The tiniest glint of a twinkling diamond set her mind to rest.

But only for a second.

Who had been in here? It was obvious that they'd come in through the window, so it wouldn't have been anyone already in the house.

Could the beast Korchenko and his minion, Stacy, have followed her this far?

It was possible, she supposed. But after they had broken into her cabin aboard ship—twice, no less, until she had the ship's captain post a guard outside her quarters—and then ransacked her hotel in New York and murdered that poor woman, she'd carefully laid a false trail and headed south. She'd even found a tallish, redheaded whore down on her luck, and given the woman two dresses, a veil, and fifty dollars above the fare south.

She'd thought she was rid of them, thought they'd followed her decoy. She thought that she'd fooled them for good, and that they were fruitlessly turning over rocks down in New Orleans.

She was an idiot.

Korchenko was a dog, a slavering, cadaverous dog on the scent. A real hound from hell, that one.

And Stacy wasn't much better.

They made quite the pair, those two. They had obviously followed her, anyway, and they had bided their time, that was all. And now they'd hired Fargo to do their dirty work for them.

Grinding her teeth, she put things back the way they'd been—why were thieves usually so bloody sloppy?—and found nothing taken, everything had just been moved around. And then she went to the window and made sure it was closed all the way and latched tight.

There was a knock on her door.

"Franny?" Mae called. "Are you coming down? I found the scrapbook I made in Wichita!"

"With you in a minute, Mae," she called back, and allowed herself a last scowl.

Fargo. It had to be Fargo.

8

Franklin Stacy stood around the corner from the Washington Arms and checked his pocket watch again. Nine-thirty. A half hour late.

Where was that blasted boy?

He'd skin Bobby Farrell's hide if he didn't show up soon. And he meant that quite literally.

At least Fargo was safely in the hotel. He'd seen his lights come up, then seen him pass the window before he pulled the curtains. Twice, he'd seen a single shadow pass.

And he knew that Francesca Ponti was ensconced safely in Mae Purvis's house—the tiara with her, blast her gorgeous hide. It had to be there. He could think of no other place for it to be. Neither had she posted anything, save for a letter or two, or passed it to a conspirator.

Oh, he and Korchenko had been most careful about that. They had watched her like hawks all through that long ocean voyage. Damn her for seducing that idiot captain! She had him wrapped around her little finger before they were a half-day out at sea. He'd put an armed seaman at the door of her cabin after their second burglary attempt.

But she'd hidden the tiara well, too well.

It was driving him crazy.

He dearly loved Korchenko, but the man was driving him mad, too. So pompous, as if the few drops of royal blood he carried made him better than everyone else. As if that fact gave him license to verbally pummel anyone who so much as slightly disagreed with him. Or got in his way.

The rich were bad enough, Stacy thought, hugging his broad shoulders against the cold. But the royals, even the very distantly related, shirttail royals . . . oh, what overwhelming pains in the buttocks!

He checked his watch again. Nine thirty-seven.

Where was that damnable boy?

It wasn't as if Stacy, himself, could blend into a crowd. No, he could do little to no surveillance without drawing unwanted attention.

He was, after all, a remarkable-looking man, he thought with a tiny surge of pride. People remembered him wherever he went. No, he could take an initial peek at the situation, but the footwork—the manual labor, so to speak—must be left to others, like that abominable little urchin. Stacy saved himself for the more delicate matters. The dispensation of Nimble Svenson, for instance.

What an odious little man.

And there would be the child to deal with, when they were through with him. Likely this Fargo character, as well.

Oh, how he wished that the wench he'd killed in New York hadn't turned out to be some matron from Savannah! He'd strangled her from behind, in the dark, and he admitted afterwards that she hadn't really smelled like Francesca Ponti, who favored a particular lavender scent. This one had smelled faintly of carbolic.

But he had her, and that mop of red hair was in his face as she struggled, and he was so pleased—and excited—to get his garrotte about her pretty neck that he hadn't asked any questions. He hadn't even looked too hard.

Such a shame. Such a waste of energy. And so frustrating when he read the papers the next morning and found that he had murdered one Mrs. Sarah Thomas, lately widowed and the mother of two.

Well, you couldn't bake a cake without cracking a few eggs, as his sainted mother used to say. Of course, she used to say that transgressors lived in the bowels of hell, too.

Damnable woman, his mother.

He checked his watch again. Ten to ten.

He looked down the street. Nothing.

He stamped his feet against the chill seeping through his expensive shoes. He wished he'd worn gloves. It seemed far too cold for Nebraska this time of year. At least, that's what he had been told. He'd never been to this dreadful place before.

He'd been watching Fargo's windows, and just then, Fargo—at least, he assumed it was Fargo—passed them again, throwing his shadow on the shades.

Good. He was still there, still alone.

What on earth was keeping that boy?

And then he saw another shape, much smaller, pass before the shades of Fargo's room, and then vanish, as if quickly pulled back and out of sight.

Stacy's brow furrowed.

The boy.

This Fargo was better than they'd thought.

He pulled a cigar from his inside coat pocket, clipped off the end, and stuck it into his mouth. He cupped his hands around a match and lit it, puffing strongly, then started back toward the depot.

This wasn't good, but it wasn't precisely dreadful, either. Oh, Korchenko would have his drawers in a knot. He always did when anything—absolutely anything—went even the slightest bit awry. But Stacy felt sure he could handle him.

After all, they'd hired the boy to watch Francesca Ponti, just as they'd hired Fargo to steal from her. What was wrong with hiring two parties, one to keep his eye on the other?

Yes, Fargo might be insulted that they engaged the boy. However, Stacy believed that Fargo was too level-headed—and the fee they'd promised him was too enticing—to prevent his dropping the quest for the

Moldavian Crown. He only hoped that Korchenko would agree with him.

Money went a very long way in these matters, and Korchenko had certainly promised to pay enough of it.

Of course, he hadn't actually had to pay anyone yet. At least, the majority of the money had always ended up in the pockets from whence it came. Nimble Svenson and a handful of others, scattered across Europe, had all ended up quite dead, each of their fees recollected almost entirely in full.

Stacy lumbered on, shoes echoing on the boards of the sidewalks, toward the distasteful job of telling Korchenko about this latest development.

"Get away from those windows!" Fargo cried, and pulled the boy back, away from the shades.

"Sorry," Bobby said, although he didn't look very sorry at all. Actually, he looked a little belligerent. He rubbed at his arm and said nothing, though.

He was wearing Fargo's spare buckskins, the old pair that was worn paper-thin and butter-soft, and the boy looked totally ridiculous in them. Fargo hadn't laughed though. Bobby had looked as proud as a peacock when he exited the bathroom in the baggy leather suit with its rolled-up, bunched-up cuffs and sleeves and its too-big shoulders, and the pants that kept falling down.

Proud, yes. Baggy, yes. But the kid's skin was about six shades lighter.

His shaggy hair, which Fargo had taken for a dark, honey blond, was so pale in its scrubbed and pristine condition that it almost appeared white. He reminded himself to get the kid a haircut, too, once he figured out what the hell to do with him.

"Dig in," Fargo said, and pointed toward the sideboard.

He only had to say it once. Bobby lifted cover after cover, and helped himself to another thick roast beef sandwich, a big ladleful of cottage fries, a heaping helping of steaming buttered peas and carrots—Fargo was surprised that the vegetables held such appeal—and topped it off with a big glass of milk from the pitcher that Fargo had ordered. Bobby wolfed everything down as if he'd never seen food before.

Bobby was slowing down a little by the time he went back for a third helping, and Fargo decided it was time to ask a few questions. He picked up the last half of a roast beef sandwich—he'd ordered three, and Bobby had eaten two and a half of them—and sat down opposite the boy.

"I take it you were hungry," he said, smiling a little.

"Uh-huh," the boy said between bites. "Thanks, Mr. Fargo."

Bobby had picked up the "mister" business the minute he saw the food, and Fargo said, "It's just Fargo, Bobby. No 'Mister.'"

"Okay," the boy said, nodding. "Can I have some more milk, Fargo?"

Fargo reached for the pitcher and poured it for him. "Tell me about Stacy."

"The fat man?" Bobby asked. "He said he'd get me to California if'n I'd keep an eye on the fancy lady for him. Said he'd pay my train fare and meals and everything all the way, nothin' too good, private sleepin' berth and everything. Him and Mr. Korchenko, that is."

Fargo cocked a brow. "Have you met this Korchenko?"

Bobby shook his head. "Nope," he said, and took in another enormous spoonful of peas and carrots. Chewing, he said, "I only heard tell of him. Sounds real foreign don't it? The name, I mean."

Fargo nodded. "What were you supposed to watch the lady for?" he asked. "Where she went, or who she saw, or what?"

"Everything," Bobby said with a shrug. "Especially, though, I was supposed to watch that she didn't post no packages. And I was to watch and see that she didn't meet nobody strange and hand somethin' off to them. Mr. Stacy said you wasn't strange, though."

"Glad to hear it. And he didn't mention my name to you?"

"Nope. He just said that the gent in the beard was all right—that meaning you." Bobby paused between bites and said, "What's she got that Mr. Stacy don't want nobody else to have?"

Fargo ignored the question. "And that was all you were supposed to do?"

"Yeah, that's it. I report to him every night. Is there any dessert?"

Fargo rocked back in his chair, his barely touched sandwich on the plate before him. "Yeah. Sideboard, top right drawer."

Bobby beat a path to it and said, "Wow!" when he discovered the big piece of chocolate cake that Fargo had salted away. He dug right in.

Now, Fargo figured that on the surface of it, Stacy was running true. Francesca had the Moldavian Crown—at least, she was supposed to have the damned thing—and he didn't want to take any chances of her handing it off to somebody else when Fargo wasn't around to stop it. That part made perfect sense.

But once you got down below the surface, a whole new crop of questions sprang up.

Why, for instance, hadn't Stacy told Fargo about the kid?

And furthermore, why hadn't Stacy mentioned that he—and possibly this Korchenko fellow—was coming on ahead to Lincoln, when he—or they—were supposed to be waiting back in Kansas City?

Something was very fishy about the whole thing.

"Y'know," said Bobby, his lips peppered by chocolate crumbs, "I don't know what it is she's got, but Mr. Stacy told me how big it is. You know, so I could watch for a package. He said anything bigger than this." He held up his hands, fork included, and gestured an object roughly the size of a pie tin, which was bigger than the tiara, but about the shape and size of what you'd have to pack it in if you were going to mail it.

"And?" prompted Fargo.

"And I was thinkin'," Bobby sliced off another big bite and lifted it to his mouth. "If I was a lady, and I had somethin' about that size I wanted to hide real good, where nobody would find it or even think to look, I figure I'd put it in my bustle. You know, that wadded up thing that ladies wear on their—"

"I know what a bustle is," Fargo said.

Bobby opened wide, inserted the fork, and smiled at the sweetness. *"Mmmm,"* he said, his eyes closed, and took another bite before he'd chewed the first.

Suddenly, Fargo slapped a hand against his own temple. Why the hell hadn't he thought of that? Of course! He'd gone through everything in that damned room, even through the gowns in the trunks, but he'd never once felt through the actual fabric for any foreign objects.

Foreign objects? That was a laugh.

"Fargo?" asked Bobby, his small brow wrinkling. "What's the matter? You look kinda peaked all of a sudden."

"Nothing," Fargo said. "Nothing, except that I'm a dad-blasted idiot." He stood up. "You know, Bobby, I don't believe that our Mr. Franklin Stacy is entirely trustworthy."

"Me neither," the boy said, lifting his milk glass. "He give me a coin, said it was lucky, but it wasn't even in American." He sniffed derisively at the idea, then took a couple of big gulps.

Fargo held up the coin, rescued from the boy's pockets. "This one?"

"Yeah," said Bobby. "Doggone foreigners."

Fargo checked his pocket watch. Ten o'clock. He might just be able to do it if Francesca had gone back downstairs, and if she was still there talking with Mae or playing cribbage or something.

It was early yet, especially for a house like Mae Purvis's.

Not so early for ten-year-old boys, though, especially when they had practically eaten themselves into a coma. Bobby had, without warning, wound all the way down, and his head was drooping dangerously toward his plate.

"Bobby?" Fargo said.

Bobby's head jerked. "What?"

"Get to bed and get yourself some sleep," Fargo said, stepping toward the door. He hiked a thumb toward the bed. "We'll talk in the morning. I have to go out for a little while."

"Sure," the boy said, scraping out his chair. He trudged to the bedside and hopped up on the mattress. "Where you goin'?"

"Gonna see a lady about a package." Fargo opened the door and had stepped halfway through it before he thought of something.

"Bobby?" The boy was already stretched out on the covers.

"Yeah?" he answered sleepily.

"Why you want to go to California? What's out there?"

The boy yawned and scratched at his ear. "My uncle. Least, that's where he was before Ma . . . before she died."

"Stay put for right now, all right?" Fargo said softly. "And whatever you do, stay away from Stacy. This thing works out the way it should, and I'll take you to California myself."

Bobby blinked and seemed to come fully awake for just a moment. "Like partners?" he said eagerly. "For real?"

"For real," Fargo replied.

Once again, Fargo found himself in the alley behind Mae Purvis's house.

The buggies had changed since he was last here, but now there were four of them. Horses dozed in the traces or munched lazily at their feed bags, filling the alley with the comforting sound of grinding molars.

Fargo wasn't comforted, however. He had work to do.

He avoided the gate again, and wisely so. Just as he was slipping over the top of the fence, a whistling, cane-twirling gent came walking down the back sidewalk from the house and opened the gate.

Fargo held his breath. He listened to the creak of buggy springs, the gather and snap of reins, and then waited until the buggy rattled down the alley. Only then did he emerge from the bushes enough to take a look upward, toward Francesca's room.

No light leaked through the curtains. She was either still downstairs or up there, asleep.

Or with somebody.

He had to take that into consideration, too, even though the thought made him madder than sin.

Five thousand dollars, he thought to himself. *Five thousand dollars.*

But even that thought, happy as it was, didn't have the strength it once had possessed. He just plain didn't trust Stacy. Of course, he hadn't from the start, but twenty-five hundred dollars up front had a way of greasing the skids under even the most stalwart fellow's misgivings. He was curious about this Korchenko fellow, and even more curious about the crown.

Who was really the thief, here?

Nonetheless, he waited for more than twenty minutes, until he caught a glimpse of Francesca. She was downstairs, all right, in a small drawing room. He wouldn't have seen her if a man hadn't opened the door for a moment, then closed it after bowing his apology. She was still with Mae, and they were looking through one of those viewers that held two slightly different views of the same picture and made it look like you were seeing things for real. Only in sepia.

Carefully, he crept toward the drainpipe.

He was up on the roof in no time, then to her window.

It took him a few minutes to loosen the latch with his knife blade, but it opened cleanly and he slid up the window without a sound.

He opened the curtains a bit to let in some moon,

and then he turned to the trunks. He wouldn't need to see much, only feel for it.

But she had locked the damned trunks, and it took him a few more minutes to pick them.

At last, he opened them and began sorting through. The first trunk contained nothing but dresses. Some were fancy—silks and satins and beadwork—but there was nothing there but fabric and a bit of whalebone.

In the second trunk, he found it in the bustle of the second dress he searched.

"I'll be damned," he whispered as he felt it through the fabric. "I'm gonna buy that kid a pony once he gets to California," he muttered, and plucked at the frayed threads of the underside of the bustle until the tiara came free.

Even in the dim light, it glittered like a thousand stars.

He didn't take much time in admiring it, though. He grabbed a scarf from her dresser and wrapped it carefully, then tied the ends of the scarf to his belt.

Out the window, across the roof, down the drainpipe, then across the yard he went. He climbed over the fence again and made his way back up the alley toward the Washington, moving his scarf-wrapped parcel inside his shirt as he walked.

Now to figure out a good hiding place for it while he figured out what to do. Or until Francesca or Stacy decided it for him.

When he got back up to his room, the boy was sound asleep in the exact position Fargo had left him in. Fargo simply flipped the bedspread over him and let him be, then slouched down into the dark and a deep leather chair to think things over.

9

"You idiot!" Korchenko said again, and Stacy cringed. "Of all the moronic, insufferable, cretinous—"

"Enough, Vladimir," Stacy finally said. "You've made your point."

"Not soundly enough, it would seem," Korchenko spat, and sat back down. At least he was seated. That meant that the worst of it was over.

Stacy hoped so, anyway.

"I don't believe it is as dreadful as it appears, Vladimir," he said hopefully. "After all, Fargo knows nothing, and the boy knows less."

Korchenko sighed deeply. "Franklin, don't you think that Fargo can put two and two together? The man is a provincial—at least, you tell me he is—but being from the provinces doesn't necessarily equate with base stupidity. Neither," he added snidely, "does being cosmopolitan equate with cleverness."

Stacy held his tongue, but he moved to the bar. He'd be damned if he'd take a tongue lashing without a taste of brandy to soothe the wounds of Korchenko's whip.

"I'll tell you exactly what this Fargo is thinking right now," Korchenko went on. "He is thinking that we would have to be in Lincoln to hire this urchin. He is thinking that we do not trust him. He is right, of course, but that is beside the point. And he is wondering what our reason for this would be."

"You have lost me, Vladimir," said Stacy, pouring

out the brandy. He raised the bottle. "Would you care for a spot?"

"Yes, thank you," Korchenko replied with a touch of disgust in his voice. "You made a much better bartender than you do a mastermind, Franklin."

Stacy felt a surge of anger, but tamped it down. The stakes were far too high to allow Korchenko's attitude to provoke him. He poured a second glass and took it to Korchenko.

"Ah, thank you, Franklin," Korchenko said, and slowly twirled the snifter in his hands, warming it. "What I am saying," he went on, "is that your Mr. Fargo will be pondering these questions and a few more. Why hire the boy to watch the lady when we've already hired him? Why come secretly to this godforsaken town of Lincoln when we could have just as easily stayed in that pigsty town of Kansas City and waited?"

Stacy, fueled by half a snifter of brandy, snorted. "Let him wonder. So long as he retrieves the Moldavian Crown and brings it to us . . ."

"Yes," said Korchenko. "There's the rub, dear Franklin. Sometimes men who think too much can't be counted on to do what they're told." He lifted a half-smoked cigar from the ashtray and relit it. "I think you will need to be doing the legwork yourself from here on out, dear boy."

Stacy's brow furrowed. "But—"

"No more hirelings. The first thing in the morning, you will go to Fargo and tell him that we are in town."

"But Vladimir, he already knows that!"

"Yes, but this news will be taken in a much more favorable light if it comes from you, personally," Korchenko said none too patiently. "You will tell him that we hired the boy. You will lay our cards on the table, so to speak."

Stacy cocked his head and his brow knitted. "All of them?" he asked. Korchenko had gone mad! "Surely, Vladimir, you don't want me to tell him—"

Korchenko threw an elegant hand into the air, and cigar ash went flying. "Of course not, you dolt," he snarled. It was obvious that he was completely disgusted, and he was making no bones about it. "For heaven's sake, man, use your head."

The next morning, Fargo had breakfast for two brought to his room. Both plates were for Bobby, who had risen bright, early, and extremely hungry. It seemed he was making up for all those months on the street.

Leaving orders that Bobby wasn't to open the door to anybody but him, Fargo went downstairs. He was fairly certain that he was going to have some visitors this morning, and it wouldn't do for them to see the kid. Not yet.

Sure enough, he had walked no more than ten feet from the downstairs landing when Franklin Stacy, all smiles and sweating like a pig, came striding across the lobby.

"Why, Mr. Stacy!" Fargo said, feigning surprise. "What are you doing in Lincoln? I thought you were going to wait for news in Kansas City!"

"Dear me," Stacy said, huffing. "I fear I have some explaining to do. May we sit?" He gestured toward a pair of the many leather wingback chairs set about the lobby floor.

"Certainly," said Fargo, and plopped down in the nearest one, where he could keep an eye on the front doors.

"I nearly didn't recognize you," Stacy said, eyeing his clothing.

"Oh, the city suit," Fargo said casually. "When in Rome. You know."

"Yes, yes, I most assuredly do," Stacy said. He mopped at his brow.

"You were going to say?" Fargo prompted.

"Oh, yes," Stacy said. "Of course. We came ahead—Mr. Korchenko and I—in case we, that is you, that is, well, in case we could be of service. We hired a boy to follow the lady in question when you were unable to. Perhaps you've seen him?"

Fargo twisted his head. "Boy? What boy?"

Stacy seemed alarmed, but covered it quickly. "Ah. Well, perhaps he is more adept at hiding in alleyways than I thought." He cleared his throat. "Should you see him, pay him no mind."

"Okay," Fargo said, and waited.

There was a long silence, and then Stacy said, "I don't suppose that you've, that it's been possible for you to, uh . . ."

"Swipe the crown?" Fargo asked. He was getting a kick out of Stacy's discomfort. He hadn't known that a fat man could sweat so much on a brisk morning like this. Hell, it couldn't have been warmer than sixty-five in the lobby.

"Yes, precisely," Stacy replied, and had another go at his forehead with the handkerchief.

"No, not yet," Fargo lied smoothly. "Haven't got a chance to get anywhere near her room yet. In time, Mr. Stacy. All in good time. This is a pretty big prize we're after. You wouldn't want me to just go rushing in like a bull in a china shop, would you?"

"No, no!" Stacy said quickly. "Certainly not. We want you to use the utmost discretion."

From the corner of his eye, Fargo caught a glimpse of his second visitor as she walked through the front doors of the hotel. Francesca spotted them, froze, then immediately turned and went out again.

He gave no sign that he had noticed. Stacy's back was to the doors so he hadn't seen her, but his bulk and height—he stuck out from the chair, both at the sides and over the top—would have made him instantly recognizable to Francesca.

She had looked pretty damned mad, both before she saw Stacy and afterwards.

"Well, then, Mr. Fargo," Stacy said, and levered himself to his feet, "I shall leave you to it, then, shall I? Should you need us or have news, our private car is side-railed at the depot."

"You're not stopping at the hotel?" Fargo asked, more to give Francesca time to hurry down the street than because he cared where the hell Stacy and Korchenko were spending their nights. He stood up, as well.

"Oh, no," replied Stacy. "Our car is quite sufficient. All the comforts of home, as they say." He let out a humorless chuckle.

"My goodness," said Fargo. "I'd like to see that."

"And you certainly shall," said Stacy. "Sooner or later."

"Until then?" Fargo said, and stuck out his hand.

Stacy studied him. "Is this your quaint way of telling me to leave you alone until you've completed your task?" he asked.

"It is," Fargo replied.

"Very well," Stacy said rather huffily, but he took Fargo's hand and shook it.

Shaking hands with Stacy was like shaking hands with a wad of dough.

"I work alone," Fargo said. "I'm sure you understand. It wouldn't be too damn smart to let the lady in question see you traipsing in and out of my hotel, now would it?"

Stacy's lips tightened a bit, but he said, "As you wish. I only came to advise you of our presence. And, uh, let you know about the boy." He nodded his head in a curt bow, swiped at his forehead again, and said, "Good day then, Mr. Fargo."

"Be seeing you, Stacy," Fargo replied.

He watched as Stacy gained the doors and stepped out in the morning air.

Stacy stopped to put his hat on, took a long look up and down the street, and then had a word with the doorman, who immediately summoned him a hack.

Fargo waited until Stacy had climbed into the back of the hansom and set off toward the depot before he allowed himself a brief smile. Then he turned and walked across the lobby and into the dining room.

"One for breakfast, sir?" asked the headwaiter, menu in hand.

"For the moment," said Fargo. "Might be a lady joining me later on. Seat me where I can see the lobby, will you?"

The waiter picked up an extra menu and stepped forward. "Very good. Right this way, sir."

He was just making room on the table for the waiter to set down his plate—eggs, bacon, hash browns, and sausage with a side of toast and blueberry jelly—when he spied her, crossing the lobby and headed, full tilt, for the stairway.

He caught the eye of the headwaiter, who fairly sprinted from his post to catch her before she mounted the stairs. She followed him to the table, and she didn't look happy.

Of course, Fargo didn't expect her to.

Once the waiter had vacated the scene, she took a quick look around, then leaned toward him. "I believe you have something that belongs to me," she hissed.

Suddenly, those sea-green eyes of hers looked like they might be better placed in the eye sockets of a pit viper.

Fargo held his expression, though, which was, for the time being, an affable smile. "Really, Francesca?" he said innocently. "Did you leave something in my room yesterday?"

She yanked the handbag from her lap and set it on the table with a cluck hard enough to rock its legs. He suspected there was something a little more lethal than a hankie in there. The look on her face told him that he was right.

"You know damn well I didn't," she said. "I want it back. Now."

Fargo looked up, and she followed his eyes. The waiter was back, his order pad in hand. "Are you ready, Miss?" he asked.

She opened her mouth, but before she could screech at him to get away or to go pound sand down a rat hole, Fargo interceded. "The lady will have what I'm having, thank you. Isn't that right, Francesca?"

"Yes," she hissed through clenched teeth. "Just lovely."

The waiter picked up her untouched menu and melted away.

"I hope you can eat two breakfasts with a hole the size of a fist in your belly, you son of a bitch," she said.

"Now, now," Fargo said. He buttered a piece of toast. "Language."

"Where is it?" she demanded. "You had no right to sneak into my rooms. You had absolutely no right to take it!"

"Sneak into your rooms?" Fargo said, toast poised at his lips. "Why, Francesca!"

"Don't give me that innocent act any more, Mr. Skye Fargo," she said, sitting up straight and lifting that elegant nose into the air. She was even more beautiful when she was angry, if that was possible.

Fargo cocked a brow. The jig was up, but he didn't much care.

"Oh, I've known who you were for the longest time," she continued, her words clipped and her tone deadly. "Fargo P. Langtree, my backside!"

"And such a pretty backside it is, Francesca," he said.

"Up yours," she spat back.

"Temper, temper," he admonished, and took a bite of his toast. He was actually enjoying this. What could she do, shoot him right in the middle of breakfast?

She glared at him.

The waiter appeared again and slid her plate to the table top before her, but she didn't touch it. She only toyed with a fork.

"Not hungry?" Fargo asked. He was already half-way through his eggs, and he had to admit that the Washington made some mighty fine hash browns. Nice and crisp, and not too much pepper.

"Where is it?" she asked, punctuating each word. "I shall not leave until you hand it over."

"Well," Fargo began, chewing, "I don't exactly—"

"And don't try to lie again," she cut in. "I saw you talking to that odious Stacy in the lobby. I know what you're up to. If you think for one minute that you're going to—"

"Stick that fork you're playing with into your hash browns," he interrupted, gesturing with his. "They do a nice job with 'em here."

Her brows lowered, her lips tightened, and she glared at him.

Well, he supposed he'd best let her off the hook.

"I might give it back to you," he said thoughtfully, and she leaned forward. "Just might, mind you. If you tell me what in tarnation is going on. And I mean the truth."

Suspiciously, she tipped her head. "Are you telling me that you don't know?"

"I know what Stacy told me," he said, chewing. "But I'm pretty sure that most everything that came out of his mouth was a lie. If you aren't going to eat those hash browns, I'd admire to—"

She shoved the plate at him with a loud clink, and several other patrons looked up.

"Easy, girl," he said.

"You are the most exasperating creature!" she said.

"And you are about the most knock-down, drag-out, gorgeous thief I've ever met. Very high-class," he said, scraping the hash browns from her plate to his. "That makes us even, I guess." He looked up. "I mean, in extremes. I'm not nearly so pretty as you are. So, go on. Tell me, my darling Francesca. Start from the beginning."

She eyed him for a long moment, studied him, and then some of the imperiousness left her face and she softened. But only a little.

She said, "And what would make me think for a single, solitary minute that you're a man of your word? After all, you burgled my room last night. Twice! I've heard stories about you, you know. Mr. Famous shoot-first-and-ask-questions-later Skye Fargo, the infamous

Trailsman. I've heard all about your exploits. It doesn't seem to me that you're entirely trustworthy."

He smiled and gave a shrug. "Just like you, Francesca."

Something on the staircase caught his eye, something short and blond, and he suddenly stood up and threw his napkin on the table.

He started for the stairs at a fast march, leaving a startled Francesca at the table. Bobby ran smack right into him on the bottom riser.

"I thought I told you to stay upstairs," Fargo hissed.

"But there was a man!" Bobby cried, and Fargo covered the boy's mouth with his hand. He dragged the kid off the stairs and set him down toward the side of the landing.

"There was a man, Fargo!" the boy whispered when Fargo took his hand away. "Some kinda murderin' thief! He came in through the window." And then he stood up a tad straighter and added proudly, "I got him conked on the head, though. And then I trussed him up with a couple'a sash cords off'n the windows. He's good and hog-tied, yessir!"

Fargo blinked, then broke out in a smile. "Atta boy, Bobby."

"You'd better come," Bobby urged, and gave Fargo's sleeve a tug.

"All right, I've just got to—"

"You have a child with you?" asked Francesca's voice from right behind him. "And all dressed up in buckskins like the big boys wear. How quaint." She bent down to Bobby. "What's your name, young man?"

Even the very young couldn't help but be slain by Francesca's beauty, Fargo thought. Bobby looked transfixed.

Or maybe poleaxed.

"B-b-b-b—" the boy stuttered.

"Bobby," Fargo said for him. "That's Bobby Farrell, junior Trailsman, to you. And we have to go upstairs for a minute."

Francesca took a step back. "The boy was in your room?" she asked, suddenly worried.

Something was rotten, and Fargo knew it. He snaked out his arm, caught her elbow, and said in a low tone, "Come upstairs. I insist on it, Francesca, dear."

10

Fargo opened his door to find a slight and wiry man, bound hand to foot, thumping and struggling on the floor at the foot of the bed. Shards of a shattered vase were all around.

"Told you," said Bobby with a proud grin.

"Nice job, kid," said Fargo. He still had a good grip on Francesca's arm; she had tried jerking away when she saw the burglar.

The man on the floor stopped twisting against his ropes, took a look up toward Francesca, and shrugged helplessly.

"Moron," she breathed, and shot him a nasty look.

"Friend of yours?" Fargo asked.

It was pretty damned obvious that Francesca had sent this stooge to burgle Fargo's room while she kept him busy downstairs. She hadn't counted on the kid, though. She also hadn't counted on the tiara not being stashed in the room, but he didn't mention that.

"Honey," he said, "if this is the item you mentioned wanting back, you're free to take him along. That is, if you can get him untied before the sheriff's men get here. Bobby, what do you say you run down to the desk and ask them to send for—"

"Oh, all right!" Francesca cried in exasperation. "I'm tired of this ridiculous cat-and-mouse game, anyway." She waggled her finger at the man on the floor. "Imbecile," she spat. "Idiot! Being taken by a boy of eleven!"

"Ten," said Bobby.

"Ten," repeated Francesca. "Untie him and let him go, Bobby." She looked toward Fargo. "He doesn't know anything."

"What she said," piped up the trussed would-be burglar.

Bobby set to work on the ropes after Fargo gave him the go-ahead. The thief rubbed at his wrists while Bobby untied his ankles and said, "Do I still get my money, lady?"

"What on earth for?" Francesca snapped. "You've only made a mess of it, Irving."

"Irwin," the burglar said testily. "Irwin Budge. And nobody said nothin' about a kid being up here, damn it."

Irwin flung away the last scraps of the curtain sash that had bound him, and got to his feet. He stood up to Francesca—he came all the way up to her collar bones—with his hands balled into angry fists. "Listen, lady, you'd best be payin' me, or—"

Fargo grabbed him by his collar and helped him to the door, saying, "You'd best be going, Irwin, before somebody calls the authorities."

"Cheapskates!" Irwin shouted from the center of the hallway. "You people don't know what the heck you're doin'! In my day—"

Fargo slammed the door in his face.

"Well, that was interesting," he said, dusting his hands.

"Gee whiz," said Bobby, blinking.

Francesca sagged into a chair. "May I sit down?" she asked, already searching through her bag for something or other.

Fargo made a grab for it, but not before she produced a handkerchief. She looked up at him and blinked. "Oh," she said. And then she smiled. "Did you think I was going to shoot you?"

"If you wouldn't mind, I believe I'll take that gun," Fargo said, then added, "Just so you won't be tempted, Francesca."

"It was only in case of an emergency," she said. She handed over her purse, muttering, "For heaven's sake!" and Fargo relieved it of a new Smith & Wesson short-nosed pistol.

"Not exactly a lady's weapon," he said, hefting it in his hand. It was a nice one, pearl handled with a well-oiled gleam. And it was loaded.

He hadn't seen it in her rooms last night. He supposed she'd "borrowed" it from some helpless gent back at Mae Purvis's house.

"Wow," said Bobby, and made a grab for it.

"I'm not exactly a lady," Francesca admitted softly, and Fargo, who wasn't exactly in the most gentlemanly mood, didn't correct her.

"Don't touch," Fargo said to Bobby, and put the gun on the top of the chifforobe. "That ought to keep it safe for a while."

Francesca was dabbing at her temples, and Fargo waited. Bobby simply twitched and craned his neck up, toward the top of the chifforobe.

"Oh, all right," she said at last. She glanced over at the boy. "Is it all right to speak freely in front of the boy?"

Fargo nodded. "Yeah. I forgot to tell you that until recently, Bobby was in Stacy's employ. He was following you."

Francesca cocked her head. "You must be very good, young man. I didn't spot you."

"Thanks, lady," said Bobby, who still seemed to be in awe of her beauty.

"But you were wise to cut your ties to Mr. Stacy, Bobby," she continued. "He is not a very nice man. Far from it. If I were you, I would stay as far away from him as I could."

"Oh, he will," said Fargo, and tousled the boy's shaggy hair. "He's my new partner, aren't you, Bobby?"

The boy beamed and gave the fringe on his rolled-up sleeve a little flick.

Fargo sat down on the edge of the mattress, facing Francesca. "Start at the beginning."

"It's a very short story, actually," she began, sitting back. "While I was in Europe, I met a man—I hesitate to call him a gentleman—named Vladimir Korchenko. He was a member of the royal court of Moldavia."

"Where?" asked Bobby.

"A tiny monarchy at the base of the Balkans," Francesca replied.

"What's a Balkan?" Bobby asked, tucking his legs beneath him. He seemed to be relaxing. "And what's a monarchy?"

"Remind me to make sure you go back to school," Fargo said.

Bobby frowned. "You don't have to go gettin' mean about it. I was only askin'."

"And no more questions," Fargo added. "Go on, Francesca."

"A certain item came into his possession," she continued. "I believe you know the item in question?"

Fargo nodded.

"It was a fluke really, his getting his hands on it," she said with a shake of her head. "Someone turned his head for just a second too long, and, well, get it he did. He fled the country. Taking me along with him, of course."

Fargo hiked a brow. "You? Why take you?"

Francesca sighed and looked daggers at him. "Well, Korchenko wasn't the only one with ulterior motives, you know. I do have my charms . . ."

"I've noticed," cut in Fargo.

"And I've learned to use them," she said, sliding him a look that said, *and the horse you rode in on, you son of a bitch.*

Fargo didn't comment.

"I had my eye on a certain necklace worn by the crown princess," Francesca went on, "and I had almost worked my way into her good graces when that idiot stole the . . . the you-know-what."

"Moldavian Crown," said Fargo, tired of the pussy-footing. "Jesus. Who's he going to tell?" he asked, pointing to Bobby.

"I'm still tryin' to figure out what a Balkan is," Bobby said.

"See?" said Fargo. "So Korchenko grabbed the crown and you, and you both took off. I'm assuming you were his, uh . . ."

It was Francesca's turn to glance at the boy. "Girl-friend," she said primly.

"Right," said Fargo, and crossed his arms over his chest.

"You're not going to get all male on me, are you?" she asked. "Start lifting your leg on lamp posts and the like?"

Fargo didn't like the idea of anybody else laying his hands on Francesca, but what was done was done. "No," he said. "Go on. And where does Franklin Stacy come into this?"

"Stacy was with us," she said. "He and Korchenko were very chummy, to say the least. I think he may have had something to do with the robbery. He and Crown Prince Alexi were close, but not as close as he and Korchenko, if you get my drift. They gave the phrase 'thick as thieves' a whole new meaning."

Fargo nodded.

Her lips tightened momentarily. "By the time we got to Dresden, I had discovered the reason for our abrupt departure. I put that reason—oh, all right, the crown—into a hatbox and walked off the train. And yes, I know I could have returned it, Fargo. But it rather . . . well, it went against my nature."

"I'll bet it did," Fargo said. He could just imagine her, standing on that distant, foreign platform with the hatbox in her hands, the jewels on it almost glowing through it. He could imagine the adrenaline flooding her body and the thrill of making off with a king's ransom, with no one the wiser but the thieves who'd stolen it in the first place.

It must have been some kind of heady rush.

"I made my way to Paris and boarded the first ship to America," she went on. "Little did I know that Korchenko and Stacy were right behind me. They booked passage on the same ship, the rogues. Might I have a glass of water, please?"

Fargo gestured to the breakfast trays. "Bobby?"

"Sure thing," the boy replied, and hopped up to fetch it.

"Stacy and Korchenko must have been awfully sloppy," Fargo said. "A month on the same ship with you, and they still didn't find it?"

"They certainly tried," she said. Bobby handed her a glass and she thanked him, then sipped at it gratefully. "Twice, they broke into my cabin and ransacked it, turned it completely topsy-turvy. Why, I had to ask dear Captain Lucas to place an armed guard outside my door!"

Fargo ignored that "dear Captain Lucas" reference, although he was pretty certain that he hated the man, just on general principle.

He said, "They tossed your cabin twice and didn't find it?"

"Certainly not," she said smugly. "Of course, I couldn't tell anyone that I knew the burglars. I couldn't tell anyone who they were, not even Captain Lucas. It might have led to embarrassing questions."

"But they didn't find the tiara?" Fargo asked, more to the point, this time. "Where the hell did you have it stashed?"

She smiled. "I was wearing it."

Fargo cocked his head.

"Not on my head, silly," she said with a sniff. "In my bustle. I kept moving it from dress to dress, you see. They never suspected."

"I'll be a son of a bitch," Fargo muttered.

"Me, too," piped up Bobby, before he said, "See, Fargo? Told you."

"You sure did, kid," Fargo said.

"When we got to New York, they broke into my hotel," she said. "Well, I say 'they,' but it was never them, personally. It would probably be prudent to add, right here, that two men went missing on board ship. Officially, they fell overboard. However, considering the professions of those men—from what I could gather on the lower decks—they were most certainly helped over the rail. New York was a horror. And in St. Louis, the women in the room next to mine was murdered in the night."

She took another sip of water, then set the glass down. "Vladimir Korchenko is a most dangerous man, Fargo. And Stacy isn't far behind. If he has the slightest idea that you are onto him, has the merest hint that I've told you what I have, then you and this child are both in great danger. He will show neither of you the slightest bit of pity or mercy. Just what was he doing here this morning?"

"Good question," he said. "He claimed he was just checking in, but I've got a feeling that he's missing Bobby, here."

"Does he know you have him?"

Fargo shrugged. This was getting them nowhere. He said, "So why not just give the crown back to them?"

"I would be just as dead," she said. "They want no witnesses. After the business in New York City, I even considered taking it to the Moldavian Embassy and turning it in. But . . ."

She shrugged most prettily. He couldn't tell whether she was lying about nearly turning the crown in, but he suspected that she was.

"You understand the call of avarice, Fargo, I'm sure," she said. "I've read about you. All that thievery and pillage. Stolen cattle and the like."

"And Indians," broke in Bobby. "Don't forget the Indians!"

"Those stupid books are full of hogwash," Fargo spat. "Ninety percent of what they say, I never did. And the other ten percent's all cockeyed, all turned on its head six ways from seven."

Bobby stared at him as if he had just revealed himself as the biggest fibber in the entire Union, and Francesca rolled her eyes heavenward.

"Just wait until some shiny-pants city slicker decides to write one of you up," Fargo grumbled. "Then we'll see how you feel about it. And Francesca, you're gonna have to give it back."

She crossed her arms. "No. It's mine."

He smiled. "Not any more, it isn't. I'm taking it to the nearest embassy."

"You snake," she hissed. Then, haughtily, she raised her chin. "You're going to have to haul it all the way to San Francisco, then. Either that, or New York City. Take your pick. But we'll just see if you still have it by the time you get there."

He cocked a brow. "That a challenge?"

She stood up. "I believe that it was. Good day." And with that, she took her leave.

Fargo and Bobby watched her slam the door behind her. Then Bobby turned to Fargo.

"All right," the boy said. "What the heck's a Balkan?"

11

Fargo's plan was to take the train not west, but south. He figured to ride the rails back to Kansas City, pick up the Ovaro plus a horse for the kid, and then set out across country. It seemed to him that there was no way in hell that Francesca—let alone Stacy and Korchenko—would follow him when there was no possibility of the comfort of a railcar.

And so he packed up quickly, then excused himself. He made a fast trip to the front desk, where he paid his bill, then scribbled a wire to be taken to the telegrapher's office by the first available messenger. One small side trip later, and he was back to the room to pick up the kid and his bag.

He hauled them to the station, double time.

"But where's that crown doo-bob?" Bobby insisted as he trotted along beside Fargo. "I seen you pack your satchel, and you didn't bring it along when you came back to the room."

"Hurry up, kid," Fargo said, and moved a little faster.

He had changed clothes at the hotel, and so they boarded the train like father and son look-alikes, both clad in bucks, both in a big toot to get to Kansas City.

They settled into their seats. Bobby was wide-eyed at the prospect of taking a trip on a real train and kept on asking questions about how the berths pulled down, and was there any place to eat or use the outhouse on the train. The more pragmatic (and far less excitable) Fargo searched the platform through the window. So far, so good.

But after the train finally jerked into a slow crawl and left the Lincoln depot behind, Francesca, all smiles and in the flesh, came strolling in from the next car down.

Fargo groaned and cursed under his breath.

She made her way up the aisle and sat opposite him, next to Bobby.

"Hello, precious," she said.

"Thank goodness," announced Korchenko flatly.

Red-faced, Stacy entered the Pullman's drawing room and dropped into the chair opposite him. Sweat poured from his brow, and he held a hand to his chest. Running to catch trains was not his strong suit. It was not even his suit at all, come to think of it.

Korchenko, calm and dry as the Sahara, eyed him.

"Thank goodness because I managed to get back to the car in time, or thank goodness because I caught the station master?" Stacy huffed rhetorically. He didn't really want to know the answer. "One day I shall have a heart attack and die."

"We shall all die one day, Franklin," Korchenko said sagely.

Stacy glared at him. "Water?"

"Certainly, Franklin, certainly," Korchenko said, and rose to make his way across the swaying floor to the bar. He poured a water glass halfway full from the carafe and brought it to Stacy, who took it gratefully.

"You know, Franklin," Korchenko said, "you really should ease off the desserts. Stop eating all the fat on your beef. Resist bread and butter. I worry about you."

In a pig's eye, you do, thought Stacy, but he said, "Thank you, Vladimir."

His palpitations eased, and he sat back. The landscape rushed along outside the window. He had just gotten to the station master in time.

It was nothing short of a miracle that he had seen Fargo coming with the boy.

Nothing short of a miracle, too, that he had managed to arrange to have the car moved and coupled to the train mere seconds before it pulled out.

Those had to be portents of good luck to come, didn't they?

He surely hoped so.

He couldn't stand much more of this.

Oh, how he wished that they would be able to retrieve the crown, and soon! A life of sweet retirement was tantalizingly close, almost close enough to touch. He and Vladimir would go someplace nice. The south of France, perhaps, or South America. Costa Rica or Brazil. Vladimir would stop being so viperous and secretive and cranky and, well, so *Vladimir*.

Stacy would no longer be relegated to sleeping in the tiny porter's booth, although there had been nights when he was glad of it, despite the cramping in his legs long after he'd risen.

But once they had possession of the crown, things could get back to normal, only better, because they would be very rich, indeed. Vladimir would be nice for a change, civil and polite and kind, and not just on the outside.

Well, as civil and polite and kind as was possible for Vladimir.

But that was good enough for Stacy. To some extent, he actually enjoyed being treated like a dog.

Korchenko's hand came to rest briefly on Stacy's shoulder.

"A good job, old friend," Korchenko said. "Splendidly done. You are forgiven for the boy."

Stacy beamed in spite of himself.

Korchenko returned to his chair, opposite his companion. "Soon," he said, lifting his newspaper to the sounds of rattling window glass, tinkling lamp shades, and iron wheels relentlessly traveling on iron rails. "Very soon, my dear Franklin. Tonight, perhaps."

* * *

Come midday, Fargo, Francesca, and Bobby were seated in the dining car, and Bobby and Fargo were studying the menu.

Francesca was studying Fargo.

Blast him, anyway!

Figuring that he'd take the first train out, she'd raced to make it to the depot in time, and had thus left behind her trunks and most of her hand luggage, only bringing along one poor bag.

Worse than that, the sleeping berths had been sold out. She would travel first class, all right, but she'd have to sleep sitting up.

But Fargo didn't seem to have the bloody crown on him anywhere! He'd made a point of leaving her behind with his bag, on the excuse of taking young Bobby out to the platform to watch the landscape roll by. And she'd searched through his bag, checked the clothes inside, checked the lining.

Nothing.

Not a blessed thing.

He certainly wasn't wearing a bustle he could tuck it in. And Bobby didn't even have a bag.

She was at her wit's end.

Not that she let on, though. She picked up her menu and stared at it blankly, thinking black thoughts about Fargo. How could he be so utterly fabulous in bed, so handsome, so tall, so thoughtful, and so . . . so . . . so mean! Taking a poor girl's only means of support without a second thought!

All right, she'd stolen it, but possession was nine-tenths of the law, wasn't it?

Except that he had it, now.

"Fried chicken," said Bobby.

Francesca looked up to find the waiter standing beside their table.

"Can I have the potatoes and gravy, too?" Bobby whispered to Fargo.

"Bring him the whole dinner, grown-up size," Fargo said to the waiter. "With all the trimmings. And a big glass of milk," he added.

"I'd druther have a coffee," Bobby said, adding hopefully, "with some whiskey in it!"

"Milk," corrected Fargo. "You want to stunt your growth?"

Bobby shrugged.

"Francesca?" Fargo said.

She hadn't even focused on the menu. "You order for me," she said, folding the pasteboard and handing it to the waiter.

"Reckon we'll have what the kid's having," Fargo said. "Except with coffee."

Bobby scowled.

"Not a word out of you," Fargo said to him.

"You're soundin' more and more like one of them orphanage people," Bobby muttered.

"All right," an exasperated Francesca said after the waiter left them. "I give up. What did you do? Put it in the bleeding mail? I hadn't suspected you were that naive, Fargo."

He smiled at her.

The man was maddening, absolutely maddening!

Bobby piped up, "I been thinkin', Miss Francesca, and I think he put it in his—"

Fargo slapped a hand over the boy's mouth. "That'll be enough out of you, Bobby Farrell. You're too good a guesser."

"*Mmmm-mmm!*" complained Bobby against Fargo's palm.

"Good boy," said Fargo.

"Sometimes I just hate men," Francesca muttered, and turned to glare out at the passing landscape.

By three in the afternoon, Fargo had decided that just staring at Francesca wasn't enough.

Oh, she was being cold all right. He couldn't blame her, really. But Lord, how could she expect to look that way and not have every man in a ten-mile radius drooling on his boots?

As it was, every male passenger in the car was more than aware of her presence. Old men stared and stammered; young men ogled, suddenly tongue-tied; and even little boys' eyes grew round.

Old and young, the women snubbed her, he noticed. They sometimes went out of their way to "accidentally" bump her when she passed. If there hadn't been any menfolk around, and if they thought they could get away with it, they likely would have mobbed her, tarred and feathered her, and hung her from a telegraph pole, just on general principle.

Jealousy was a big female cat with long, sharp claws, Fargo thought.

Francesca took it all in stride, however. In fact, she hadn't seem to notice. It must have always been like this for her.

At three-thirty, she got up to stretch her legs. The matron behind them scowled at her, and the farmer's wife across the aisle clicked her knitting needles together fiercely.

"Mind if I come with, Francesca?" Fargo asked, rising from his seat, too.

"Of course not," she said.

Bobby started to get up as well, but Fargo said, "You stay put, kid, and watch the seats. Keep an eye on the bags, while you're at it."

"Hey!" the boy grumbled. "I thought we was partners."

"Partners watch each other's things," Fargo said.

Bobby brightened a little. "Oh. Okay."

"Be back in a shake," said Fargo with a tip of his hat, before he took it off and tossed it up into the overhead. Hatless, he followed Francesca down the aisle and out onto the little platform between cars.

He closed the door behind them and took her arm. "Look, I'm sorry, Francesca," he began, "but the damned crown has to go back where it belongs. That's all there is to it."

In reply, she turned, wrapped her arms around his neck, and kissed him deeply.

It took him completely off guard—stunned him actually—but not for long. He returned her kiss while the wind whipped and rushed around them, cinders pinged into his cheek, and the clatter and roar of the rails urged him on.

"Baggage car," she murmured into his ear after she gave it a little lick, and that was all he needed to hear. Quickly, his erection stiffly thumping his belly, he led her back through several more cars to the baggage car and threw the door closed behind them.

In the dim interior, lit only by thin, mote-filled strips of light let in by the car's side boards, he heard the rustle of her skirts as she raised them, saw a tantalizing glimpse of thigh and another of hip, saw her reach for him.

He went willingly.

He took her atop a steamer trunk, and took her hard.

She let out a gasp when he entered her, a gasp and his name. She wriggled against him and slid her bare thighs up his to lock her ankles behind his back. He grabbed hold of her ass, the perfect flesh covered in gooseflesh from the chill, or maybe from what they were doing.

He didn't know.

All he knew was that she was wet and tight and more than enthusiastic, and that she knew exactly what she was doing.

He stroked into her fast, then slow, then fast again, and she met him thrust for thrust. Eagerly, he listened to the little sounds she made: the hissed intakes of air, the soft squeals, the tiny groans and growls. There was a fire kindling in his belly as well, a fire that was about to roar into an all-consuming blaze.

Her fingers clawed the back of his neck, ripped at the laces on his shirt to find the flesh beneath. Her teeth nipped at his jawline, her tongue made warm circles and swipes on his throat.

His hands were all over her, tracing the line of a breast through too many layers of fabric, sweeping down the small of her back, cupping her head while his tongue lapped at her ears. His fingers trailed down that long, pale throat as he kissed the delicate collarbones, then tongued her cleavage.

And just when he was thinking that he couldn't possibly hold it back any longer, she suddenly craned her neck back and gave him a gigantic squeeze with her internal muscles.

It was like abruptly pouring a bucket of kerosene on an open fire, and he couldn't have stopped the roaring conflagration even if he'd tried.

As one, they exploded into an ecstasy that seemed to go on and on and on.

At last, Fargo rolled off of her, feeling as if he'd been shot out of a cannon and had landed, miraculously, on a cloud.

"Jesus, Francesca," he said, running a sleeve over his sweating brow.

She let her skirts down. "Lord, Fargo, you're good," she said, panting and slit-eyed. "I almost don't mind that you stole my crown."

That again.

Fargo reached down and pulled up his britches. Fastening them, he said, "Honey, you picked a swell time to bring that up again."

"Should I have brought it up before we made love?" she asked with a note of humor in her voice. Then softly, she put her hand to his cheek. "I am what I am, darling Fargo. What are we going to do about tonight?"

Fargo cocked a brow. "Tonight?"

"Some weasel—I'm assuming it was you—got the last sleeping berth. I am without a place to lay my head, unless you wish to count sitting up in a first-class seat as sleeping," she said.

He wished he could see her face clearly. He was imagining a very pretty pout.

"Oh, I reckon we could find you a place to snooze," he said, and put his arm around her.

"We'll have to be very quiet," she whispered.

"We can manage," he said.

"Fargo, darling?" she murmured, curling against his

side. He felt a tiny breeze against his cheek as she fluttered her lashes. "I would surely sleep better tonight if I knew where you put that—"

"Hush," he said, and kissed her.

12

By four-thirty, Fargo was dozing in his seat, his hat pulled low over his eyes. Bobby was curled up beside him, one arm artlessly dangling in the aisle, his mouth open, his eyes closed.

They certainly made a picture, Francesca mused, smiling just a little despite herself. The two of them tugged at her heartstrings in a new manner, a manner for which she didn't much care. It made her feel all warm on the inside, made her feel like stirring up a turkey dinner, made her feel like humming and making soap and darning socks.

Good God, she thought with a shake of her head. What was wrong with her?

Quietly, she slipped away, stepping carefully over Fargo's outstretched legs.

She walked out the back of the car, then through several more, including the baggage car where she and Fargo had played earlier that afternoon, back through the caboose, and finally came to the Pullman.

She stood for several moments on the little platform outside its front door. Then she stood erect, squared her shoulders, and knocked at the glass.

Stacy answered, the pig.

His initial look of surprise was swiftly replaced by a glare.

She knew he hated her. She had committed the cardinal sin of replacing him, however briefly, in Korchenko's affections.

She nodded. "Franklin," she said.

"Miss Ponti," he replied. His baritone voice was clipped and full of repressed anger. His color was rising, too, seeping red and hot-pink up into his fat cheeks.

Francesca imagined that she'd best get inside before he lost all control and threw her beneath the car's wheels.

"May I come in?" she asked. She knew Korchenko would be in. He was always in. He wouldn't want to dirty his shoes with American soil.

Stacy didn't answer. He simply moved his great bulk out of the way, just enough for her to squeeze past. Which she did, registering her distaste with a small grunt.

She entered the drawing room just as Stacy announced her presence.

Korchenko looked up. If he was surprised to see her, he hid it well. He simply rose, put down his book, and folded his arms.

"My goodness," he said evenly. "Francesca Ponti. I must say, you're looking well."

"And you, Vladimir," she replied dryly. "I believe you've lost a little color."

One corner of his mouth crooked into a half-smile. "Always the wag, Francesca." He swept an arm toward the chair opposite the one he'd just vacated.

She sat down primly, hands in her lap, ankles crossed, skirts smoothed.

He sat, too. Stacy, glowering, remained standing and silent.

"So," began Vladimir as he picked up his cigar. "You have lost the crown."

Francesca didn't display any surprise. She had none to show. Vladimir would have known it was the only reason she would come to him.

"I have," she said.

"Does Fargo have it on his person?" Vladimir asked. He signaled to Stacy to bring them something or other from the bar.

"Don't you know?" she asked. "He was your man, after all."

"I was led to believe so, yes," Vladimir replied. He threw a brief scowl in Stacy's direction. "But one can never tell unless push comes to shove, can one? This is the correct phrase, is it not?"

And it had come to that, she supposed. She sighed. "Correct, Vladimir. And no, I suspect one can't. Thank you, Franklin."

She accepted the sherry glass from Stacy's tray, and waited for Korchenko to take his. And then waited for him to take a sip before she drank. At least he hadn't tried to poison her. Yet.

As if reading her thoughts, Korchenko said, "I should be very cross with you, you know."

"But you're not?" she said, hiking one brow.

"Yes, but not so cross as I was," he replied. "It does my heart a world of good to see you slapped to the ground by this . . . saddle tramp." He turned toward Franklin Stacy. "This is the correct phrase as well, is it not, Franklin?"

Franklin, momentarily back in Korchenko's good graces, smirked smugly. "That is precisely correct, Vladimir."

Francesca closed her eyes. It was either that or roll them. "You seem very intent on correct phraseology, Vladimir. And I would hardly call it a fatal blow," she said after a moment. "I am, after all, traveling with him."

"And that whelp," Stacy grumbled.

Korchenko waved his hand. "Forget about the boy, Franklin. He is nothing. But Fargo, he is another matter entirely." He turned to Francesca. "I take it, my dear, that you have not discovered the whereabouts of the crown?"

"That would be rather obvious, Vladimir," she replied. "I should hardly come to you if I knew where it was."

Vladimir sniffed. "He has not posted it?"

"No."

"Crated and shipped it?"

"No."

"Left it with a comrade?"

"Not to my knowledge."

"Then he carries it with him."

Francesca shook her head. "If he does carry it, I haven't found it. I've searched Fargo's satchel to no avail, and the boy carries no luggage at all."

Korchenko stroked his chin. "Clever, this Fargo, very clever. Perhaps we have underestimated him, eh, Franklin?"

Stacy said nothing.

"He has hidden it elsewhere on the train, then," Korchenko said after a few moments of thought. "That is the only place it can be, or so would say deductive reasoning." Then he leaned back in his chair. "So many places to search, so many nooks and crannies!" he cried, spreading his hands. "I ask you, Francesca: Can it possibly be worth the trouble?"

She stared at him flatly.

He smiled.

"And what is it that you want?" he asked. "Besides your life, that is."

It was her turn to smile.

"If we might speak freely, Vladimir?" she said, then slid her glance toward Stacy. "Alone?"

"Certainly, my dear," he said. "Franklin, would you please give us some privacy?"

Stacy frowned. "What?"

"If you wouldn't mind stepping outside for a moment?" Korchenko repeated.

Francesca had to hand it to Korchenko. He could slice to the bone with less effort and fewer words than most men, and draw substantially more blood. Stacy looked positively flummoxed.

He nodded a curt bow and left them.

They both heard the door slam behind him.

"Ah, my dear," Vladimir said with a sigh, "how I have missed simply gazing upon your angelic face."

"And how I have missed your money and connections, Vladimir," she replied.

He laughed, dry and brittle. "Always to the point. Lovely, just lovely."

She leaned forward and took his hand in hers. "Shall we get down to brass tacks?"

He squeezed her hand, holding it too tightly for a moment, but she resisted the urge to withdraw. It was like being squeezed by a handful of twigs; twigs with a life of their own. How could she ever have let this man make love to her?

But she smiled steadily. She looked him straight in the eye, and purred, "Yes, let's. Do you remember Vienna, Vladimir? Two years ago in the winter?"

A smile slowly spread across his cadaverous face. "Yes, indeed. The Countess's ruby necklace. How could I forget?"

"I think," Francesca said, "that this is much the same."

Come six o'clock, while Fargo and Francesca and Bobby were in the dining car partaking of a roast beef dinner, Stacy was pacing back and forth in the Pullman's drawing room.

Midnight! Why on earth did he have to wait until midnight to go searching for the Moldavian Crown? Everyone would surely be sleep by ten, and sawing the proverbial logs by ten-thirty. But no, Korchenko insisted that he not enter the sleeping car until after the stroke of twelve.

Bah.

And of course, Korchenko wouldn't do it himself. Never mind that Stacy was so broad of beam that his hips and arms brushed against the berths and rustled the curtains on either side. Never mind that there was absolutely no way he could be in the smallest part stealthy.

It was ridiculous.

And that woman, coming to crawl because she'd

lost what she'd stolen from them; that was even more ridiculous! And she'd demanded half of the profit! What nerve, what gall!

If he'd been Vladimir, he would have beheaded her on the spot.

Of course, knowing Korchenko, he probably had something quite interesting planned for her later on. He wouldn't give up his spoils that easily.

There was a rap on the glass of the car's front door, and he called, "Enter!"

Two porters came in, both bearing trays. Stacy rubbed his hands together. At least there was food in which to drown his misgivings.

"Vladimir!" he called. "Dinner has arrived."

The porters laid out Stacy and Korchenko's supper on the sideboard. There was prime rib cooked just the way he liked it, pink, juicy, and bloody red in the center, along with garlic potatoes swimming in butter.

He let the aroma tickle his nose.

A lovely succotash filled a silver bowl, slivered almonds mixed with green beans cut french-style filled another, and butter melted yellow over the crown of a steaming head of cauliflower. Warm, crusty fresh rolls crowded a basket set betwixt pots of whipped butter and pots of jelly.

He lifted the top off another dish, and found two large servings of strawberry-and-apple crumble topped with whipped cream, the dishes set in a bowl of shaved ice to keep them chilled.

"Delightful," he said, feeling the saliva rush to fill his eager mouth. He placed a coin in each of the men's outstretched hands.

The first one took his coin, bowed, and exited, but the second one—Vladimir's snitch—stayed, hands clasped behind his back, rocking on his heels.

"Vladimir!" Stacy called again.

"I heard you the first time," Korchenko said. He entered the drawing room from the bathroom, wrapped in a plush robe, wearing slippers, and rubbing at his wet and graying head with a towel.

"Ah," he said when he saw the porter. "Mr. Jenkins. What have you to report?"

"The feller and the boy have got berths in first class," the porter replied. "Seven A and Seven B. The lady ain't got one."

"Poor thing," lamented Korchenko, and sniffed the roast beef. "How degrading to have to sleep in one's chair."

Stacy didn't care if the bitch was comfortable or not. He snagged a chunk of potato off the platter and popped it into his mouth. Delicious! He licked his fingers.

"Oh, for heaven's sake, man," Korchenko grumbled. "Control yourself."

Stacy shrugged.

"Oh, I doubt she'll be sleepin' on anything hard tonight," the porter said, wiggling his eyebrows, " 'less it's the feller."

Korchenko hiked a regal brow. "Do tell."

The porter leaned toward Korchenko's ear, and Stacy took the liberty of snatching a warm roll which he crammed into his mouth, whole.

"Seems one'a the other fellers seen them goin' in the baggage car this afternoon," the porter said, a leer on his face. "Seems he sort of crawled up top it and took a peek."

"And?" Korchenko asked.

"Well," the porter said, sliding a glance left, then right, "it seems they was goin' at it like a couple'a cur dogs in heat."

Korchenko tipped his head. "Really."

Not everything was going as Korchenko had planned, Stacy thought a tad giddily as he chewed. And it was quite obvious that Francesca hadn't told him this choice little tidbit. This was excellent. Korchenko needed a little waking up. He needed to get the wench out of his system for good and all.

"I imagine your chum's peek turned into quite a long look, indeed," Korchenko said thoughtfully and without a hint of emotion.

Odd, thought Stacy, but then, Korchenko was most skilled at hiding his emotions.

"Oh, that it did, Mister," the porter said, and winked.

"Franklin?" said Korchenko.

Stacy swallowed hastily. "Certainly, Vladimir," he replied. He produced yet another coin, this one a five-dollar gold piece, from his pocket. He flipped it to the porter.

Jenkins caught it in midair, bit down on it and, satisfied, stuck it into his pocket.

"That will be all, Jenkins," Korchenko said. "For now."

"Real good, sir," the man said nodding, and then took his leave.

"Honestly," Korchenko grumbled, as he began to fill his plate. Stacy was not far behind. The roll had only whetted his appetite.

Stacy fully expected a lengthy diatribe on the general untrustworthiness of women in general and Francesca Ponti in particular, but he was to be disappointed.

"You would think," Korchenko said, ignoring the Francesca and Fargo matter entirely, "that these beastly people would be able to speak their own bloody language. Why, I speak four languages in addition to my own, and I speak each and every one of them far better than these natives. Someone should shoot them if for nothing but respect for their mother tongue."

Stacy was too busy chewing to answer.

It was excellent prime rib: juicy, tender, and flavorful. And it took his mind away from his copious problems.

13

By nine-thirty, people were beginning to pull down their berths with the aid of the porters. Fargo wasn't tired yet, not by a long shot, and the train kept stopping at every little wide spot in the road.

"Dining car still open?" he asked a passing porter, laden with bed linen.

The man replied, "Till ten, sir. You want I should pull down your berth?"

Francesca stood up, and Fargo and Bobby followed suit. "By all means," Fargo said, and flipped the man a coin.

You were supposed to tip for these small services, and he didn't feel much like pulling the heavy berths down himself, let alone making up the mattresses.

Single file, they walked to the dining car, and Fargo found himself admiring the sway of Francesca's lovely backside, and imaging it naked beneath the bustle.

He smirked, then reminded himself that he was here to get a job done. Anything extra—that meaning Francesca—was just icing on the cake.

Icing laced with arsenic, perhaps.

He knew that despite her pretense, she wasn't going to give up on the crown so easily. He knew she'd searched his valise. He'd left the car on purpose so that she could. She was likely going about half-crazy, wondering where he'd put it. And this afternoon, while he was pretending to doze, she'd left for about a half hour and come back looking very determined.

Dollars to doughnuts, she'd made some sort of a deal with Korchenko and Stacy.

Oh, he knew about their Pullman. He'd known ever since about five or six stops back, when he'd climbed down off the train to stretch his legs on the platform and spotted it hooked to their train, back behind the caboose. He had to hand it to those fellows. They were pretty quick on the uptake.

But they were deadly, too. He couldn't allow himself to forget that.

When they reached the dining car, Fargo ordered coffee for himself and Francesca and a piece of chocolate cake and a glass of milk for Bobby. The kid was already drowsy. Fargo figured he'd nod off as soon as his head hit the pillow.

Fargo and Francesca made small talk—during which they played footsie under the table—and drank their coffee, and by ten, when the dining car was ready to close down, they were ready to leave for greener—and infinitely more entertaining—pastures.

Bobby had fallen asleep at the table, his cake half-eaten. Fargo picked him up and carried him back up to the first-class car.

It looked quite different, now. All the berths had been pulled down and made up, and only two rows of seats at the rear, mostly filled with passengers trying to get halfway comfortable for the night, were left set up.

"There but for the grace of God go I," Francesca muttered as they passed them.

Fargo found their berths, and started to roll Bobby into the upper of the two.

Francesca stopped him, though. "What if he rolls out in his sleep?" she asked, then added in a low tone, "It's a very long drop to the floor for such a little boy, Fargo."

"Going maternal on me?" Fargo asked, then grinned when she looked surprised.

She rolled her eyes at him. "Oh, stick him on the floor for all I care."

"Right," said Fargo, and tucked Bobby safely into the lower berth. For good measure, he put his satchel at the boy's feet, then on second thought, threw in his hat, too. No sense in getting it squashed, up top. He figured he and Francesca were going to do a good bit of thrashing around.

Eschewing the ladder, he gave Francesca a boost up. She felt good beneath his hands.

"Can you give me a few minutes, Fargo?" she asked sweetly, and batted her eyes.

"Sure can," he said. "Believe I'll go stand outside for a bit. Cool my bones off."

"Don't get them too chilly," she said, and closed the curtains.

Slowly, Fargo walked to the end of the car, gently elbowing people in various stages of undress aside, and stepped out, onto the deck and into a world of noise and whipping wind.

Once he determined that the coast was clear, he deftly swung himself out to the side, over the swiftly passing ground, and to the service ladder on the side of the car.

Cold wind lashed him as he climbed up to the roof, and a colder, more insistent blast hit him when he reached the top. It couldn't be helped, though.

He made his way to the end of the car, the wind pushing relentlessly at his back as he jumped to the roof of the next, and so on, until at last he padded over the roof of the caboose. The Pullman had been hitched on at the last minute, and was therefore last in the hookup.

After carefully dangling upside down to check through the windows of the caboose, he satisfied himself that none of the crew were present. Then he climbed down the ladder and swung himself to the little platform at the front of the private car.

He crouched there, hugging his shoulders. The wind had bitten through his bucks, and it took him a minute to get his circulation going again. And all the time that he was willing his blood to move, to warm him up, he listened at the door.

109

There was nothing he could make sense of.

Not a blessed discernable word, nothing except for the relentless clatter of wheels on tracks. A least they were so far back from the engine that he didn't have to worry about flying cinders pinging him right and left.

They were in there, though. Light blared from the car's windows, and he could just make out the low murmur of conversation.

He couldn't make out any words, however.

But at least they were both still in the car.

He moved back, to the caboose's platform, and leaned down between the two. The train must be on an imperceptible downhill grade, because there was no tension whatsoever on the coupler.

He let himself down a little farther, then reached for it.

The big pin came out with little effort, as those things went, and he watched as slowly the Pullman began to separate from the train. Once there was a gap of a foot or two between the cars, he tossed the pin out into the swiftly passing brush.

Then he got to his feet and gave a satisfied bat to his hands. There was about ten feet between the cars now. Downhill grade notwithstanding, they had bid adieu to Masters Stacy and Korchenko, for at least the time being.

He smiled, checked the caboose again—there was still no one inside—swung himself up on the ladder once more, then climbed to the roof of the caboose.

He wished he could see Stacy's face.

No, he wished he could see Francesca's.

Come to think of it, he thought with a grin, he would.

He kept moving forward, into the biting wind, over the roofs of the cars.

Francesca waited for him.

This was a devilish sort of business, she mused, sleeping with the man whom you were about to rob.

Not that she hadn't done it before. Actually, as these things went, it was a fairly common occurrence in her line of work.

But still, this was Fargo. And he was different. He wasn't one of her usual pasty, flabby, society snobs. He was smart as a whip, and he used that intelligence every bit as cleverly as she used hers.

And to make matters worse, he was as far from pasty and flabby as a man could possibly be. That he was an excellent lover went without saying. That was one area where the books had been right, for what little they intimated.

Sighing, she slithered under the sheets, feeling the cool, smooth linens slide against her bare skin. No modest nightgowns when it came to bedding down with Fargo, nor those flimsy silks she sometimes wore when it came down to the grand seduction of some potbellied mogul who had more money than sense, more lust than finesse. No, with Fargo, she wanted to be as naked and free as the day she was born.

He did, after all, make her feel almost brand-new.

She almost felt guilty about going behind his back to Korchenko and Stacy.

Almost.

"Can I come in?" said a familiar voice from outside the curtains, and she smiled as a rush of gooseflesh swept her body.

Fargo.

"It's your berth, darling," she said.

His hand opened the curtains and he sat down on the edge of the lower berth to pull off his boots. She reached down from above and touched his arm. "You're freezing!" she said.

"It's cold outside."

She added, "Well, come in here and let me warm you, pet."

He swung his legs up and pulled the curtains closed behind him. "Nothing I'd admire more," he whispered, and kissed her on the neck.

Another flood of gooseflesh hurried down her body.

She plucked at his shirt lacings.

He kissed her again, this time on the lips, and slid the bedclothes from her body. His hand covered her breast and tweaked the nipple, and although she hadn't thought they could grow any harder, they did, almost to the point of pain.

It was a sweet, sweet pain, though.

"Get undressed," she murmured against his lips. "I want you now. This minute."

In the dark, he chuckled.

"Yes ma'am," he said, and his voice was so rich and deep that it made her shiver. "Right away, ma'am." And for a moment he eased way from her.

She felt him rustling the covers as he struggled to slip out of his clothes in the crowded space. Train berths, after all, were meant for one person, and only when that one person didn't intend to roll over or toss and turn very much.

But at last he stretched out beside her. She could feel every inch of his skin from head to toe, and as he laid his hand on the flat of her belly, her fingers traveled over his back and shoulders, feeling all those wonderful hard angles, all that tensed muscle. He was like living steel covered in warm flesh.

He could rip me apart with his bare hands, she thought with a thrill, and felt a tiny gush of moisture between her legs.

Which his fingers immediately delved into.

Unbidden, she let out a little gasp of surprised pleasure.

He kissed her, warm and firm. Their lips opened and she took his tongue into her mouth, sucked it, clung to it, as his fingers teased her below. His beard tickled her and felt incredibly erotic against her face, all at once.

Her hand went to his shaft and grasped its thickness. He was already fully erect, and so big that the ring of her fingers didn't meet when she held him.

She began to stroke him, to glide her fingers up and down, to slide her palm along him, and picked

112

up that first droplet of moisture and spread it. She felt the silky skin stretched over the rock-hardness beneath.

He slipped his knee between her legs, and she more than willingly spread them for him. "Yes," she whispered. "Yes, Fargo."

He slid into her, effortlessly and smoothly, and she hissed again at the sensation. She had been with many men, but the feeling of Fargo inside her was like no other.

Without thinking, she curled her legs around his hips and locked her ankles behind his thighs.

He dipped his head and took one of her nipples into his mouth, teasing it with his teeth so that she felt as if there were a wire of bright silver connecting her breast to her groin, as if it were charged with some sort of heavenly fire.

He was deep inside her, but hadn't moved yet, and still, she felt herself about to topple over the edge. "Fargo," she whispered, her neck arched, her eyes half-closed. "Fargo."

And then he drew back, his teeth still on one nipple, his fingers sliding over the other, taking it, twisting it to mimic the actions of his teeth.

He drew nearly out, and the slow sensation of it, combined with what he was doing to her nipples, was nearly too much to handle.

But that was nothing compared to what happened next. He suddenly drove forward, burying himself, and she exploded, losing control of her arms and legs for a moment, thrashing wildly beneath him.

The next thing she knew, his hand was covering her mouth and she could just see him through the darkness, smiling at her. He was still inside her, as big as ever, and her internal muscles squeezed him rhythmically in involuntary contractions.

"What . . ." she began breathlessly. "What did you do?"

"Feller's got to have some secrets," he whispered, and kissed her nose. "Ready?"

He was quite a fellow, indeed, this Fargo. Still panting slightly, she smiled. "Ready for anything, dearest."

He began to move, and after a moment, she moved with him.

14

Somewhere, in that moment of fire and bliss and release, Fargo sensed that something was wrong. The train seemed to jolt beneath him, beneath Francesca, but he couldn't be certain. Making love to her on a barreling train was a heady experience in itself, but was the earth itself supposed to move beneath the rails?

He didn't think so.

He forced himself to open his eyes as the last, incredibly sweet effects of his climax washed through his body, and pulled the curtains slightly ajar.

"What?"

"*Shh,*" said Fargo, and placed his fingers over her lips.

If that jolt had been the result of their lovemaking, then the whole car must have been in on it.

Several passengers, puzzled to suddenly find themselves not only awake, but on the cold, rough floor, were picking themselves up and rubbing at their backsides or heads. Up and down the row, curtains were coming open and people, their eyes still slitted with sleep, peered out and ground their palms into their eyes.

A porter came hurrying down the aisle, helping people up and stepping over others, and Fargo caught his shoulder.

"What the devil's going on?" he asked.

The porter shook his head. "I'm sure it's all right,

sir," he said, and Fargo instantly knew that the man knew little more than he did.

"Did we hit something?" Fargo insisted. They might have run smack into a herd of cattle, after all. Such things were not unknown.

"No, it came from the back of the train," the porter said, and tried to shake free his arm. Fargo wasn't letting go. "We were slowing down to take on water, and something slammed into us," the man said patiently, then looked at his arm—and Fargo's hand on it. "Sir, do you mind?"

Fargo loosed his grip. "Sorry," he said, and the porter hurried on down to the tail of the car and slipped through the door.

"Shit," Fargo hissed as he let the curtains swing closed behind him.

"What happened?" breathed Francesca. Her cheeks were still flushed with her second climax of the evening. Fargo had wanted to make it three.

And now this.

Of all the lousy luck!

"Nothing, honey," he soothed, even though he didn't feel especially soothing. "Something hit us, that's all. Or we hit it. No damage done." He reached for his bucks and his boots.

"Where are you going?" she asked, her brows knitted prettily.

"Gonna go and have a look-see," he said as he pulled up his britches, snatched up his boots and his shirt, and slithered to the floor of the car. "I'll be back."

He sat down on the edge of Bobby's berth and began to tug on his boots.

"You okay, kid?" he asked, parting the curtains as another distraught, half-clothed passenger jostled past his knees.

"What happened?" Bobby asked sleepily, propping himself on both elbows. And then he peeked out the curtains and brightened a bit, asking eagerly, "Was there a wreck?"

Fargo tousled the boy's hair. "No such luck," he

said with a grin. "Don't worry about it. Go back to sleep."

"But—"

"Sleep," Fargo said. "Or at least, stay put if you can't doze off. There are too many folks milling around out here. You'll get trampled."

By the time he'd gotten his boots on and stood up and put on his shirt, the train had come to a standstill and it looked—and sounded—like just about everyone in the car was awake, if not in the aisle.

Through the close-knit, yammering crowd, he shouldered his way down to the end and stepped outside, into the brisk air. Leaning off the little platform, he saw personnel with lanterns scurrying along toward the train's tail. More than a few passengers, mostly men, had already detrained and were wandering along in the wake of the lanterns, following the lights and the shouts.

"Son of a bitch," Fargo muttered, and hopped down off the train, into the throng from first, second, and third class.

He knew exactly what had hit them. It was undoubtedly that mother of a Pullman. Why did this stretch of track have to be on a downhill grade? And why the hell had they had to stop for water before the tracks started uphill again?

He hoped the impact had broken both Stacy's and Korchenko's necks.

Sure enough, by the time he reached the caboose, the crew had already found a new pin somewhere and re-attached the Pullman.

"Anybody hurt?" he asked a passing conductor.

"Naw," the man said. "Just a little shook up. I can't figure what happened. How does a metal pin like that break smack in two?"

When Fargo looked puzzled—or hoped that he did—the conductor added, "The pin come out. The pin that couples the cars." He made a circle with the fingers of one hand, then stuck his index finger through it. "You know, like that."

"Ah," said Fargo. He flicked his gaze over the conductor's shoulder, toward the Pullman. No signs of life. Maybe Stacy and Korchenko were too shook up to be of any bother tonight.

He hoped so.

"Damn thing come out or busted or somethin'," the conductor went on. "I been with the Union Pacific for seven years, and never heard of such a thing happening. Beats me how it could have, 'less somebody pulled it out a-purpose."

Fargo tried to look innocent. "Why would anybody do that?"

"Beats me," the man repeated.

And just then, over the conductor's shoulder, Fargo saw Stacy. He was standing off about thirty feet at the Pullman's side. Stacy glared at him, his hands wadded into righteous fists at his sides, slowly beating against his thighs.

He didn't look the least bit concussed. He only looked mad.

"It doesn't beat him," Fargo muttered.

"What say?" the conductor asked.

"Nothing," Fargo said, and patted him on the shoulder. "Just glad nobody was hurt." Stacy was still staring daggers at him.

"Yessir, that's a blessing," the man replied, tipped his cap, and started to walk toward the front of the train, patting the cars here and there as if the train were a horse he was calming.

Which, aside from the men milling around him, left Fargo standing alone.

Stacy moved toward him.

Fargo held his ground, quickly flipping through his mental notes. He had to handle this situation, and quickly.

"Fargo," said Stacy, once they were nose to nose. Stacy'd have to stay civil, Fargo figured. There were too many people close at hand.

"Mr. Stacy," said Fargo, hoping that something re-

118

sembling happy surprise registered on his face. "I'm surprised to see you."

"I'll just bet you are," rumbled Stacy with an icy glare.

Fargo didn't let it get to him. He said, "I thought you'd be back in Lincoln, waiting. I set off in something of a rush, after all."

Stacy seemed to be taken aback by this, by Fargo's feigned innocence in the matter, but it only took him a second to get himself back on track.

"You have something that belongs to me," he said in that deep voice. It seemed to come up from the earth itself, Fargo thought, from some low, evil place.

Fargo didn't let it intimidate him, though, because Stacy had made a mistake. He'd just laid all his cards on the table. There was no need for subterfuge, now, not on any count.

Fargo crossed his arms and hiked a brow. "I thought it belonged to your employer."

Stacy's face darkened. "We wish to have it back, Mr. Fargo. Now."

Fargo shook his head slowly. "Now, I don't believe that's an option, there, Stacy. See, I've got it on good authority that the crown wasn't yours—or your boss's—to begin with. Seems like I'm dealing with a whole passel of thieves, and I don't much cotton to it. Don't cotton to it at all, in fact." He paused a moment to purse his lips thoughtfully. "No, I think I'd best get that little bauble back to its rightful owners."

"Mr. Fargo, you were hired to do a job!" Stacy sputtered. "You agreed to do it. You accepted our earnest money!"

From up ahead came the familiar call of "All aboard! All aboard!" Fargo turned to see lanterns swinging past him as conductors and porters ushered people back onto the train. He began to follow, then turned again to Stacy, who hadn't budged.

"By the way, Mr. Stacy," he called with a short wave of his hand, "I quit. Convey that to your buddy, will you?"

"Someone cut loose our *what*?" Francesca asked. She was fully if hastily dressed, and standing in the narrow aisle between berths.

Molly Blodgett, a cheery North Dakota farmer's wife en route to Wichita, Kansas, who had, in the space of ten minutes, become Francesca's new best friend, said, "Our Pullman. I mean, the one our train was towing. Isn't that the craziest thing? Why would somebody want to leave those poor people stranded? Of course," she added, twisting her head, "I don't suppose they can actually be poor, can they? I mean, riding in a private car and all. They'd be the opposite of poor, now, wouldn't they? Still, it seems sort of—"

"Fargo," muttered Francesca through clenched teeth. That rat bastard!

"Cargo?" Molly said, misunderstanding. "I don't think anybody said anything about any cargo. And don't you have to be on a ship to call it that? Course, I'll bet you've been on a ship before," she added. "You're so . . . worldly, you know?"

But Francesca didn't take in the half of it. She was thinking evil thoughts about Fargo. How in the devil had he known that Korchenko and Stacy were back there? And why had he cut their car loose, as Molly had so eloquently put it?

He must know, damn it. He must have figured out that she had been back there, that she had talked to them. Blast him, anyway!

And what was he doing out there right now, while she was standing here like an idiot, listening to Molly Blodgett blather on about ships and Europe and husking corn and planting potatoes?

Oh, this was his handiwork, all right. No doubt about it.

". . . been to France," Molly was saying.

The train lurched. They were underway again, albeit at a snail's pace. She supposed they were moving ahead to the water stop that Molly had mentioned earlier.

"France?" she asked, just to be polite. One never

knew when a compatriot would come in handy, and Molly seemed to desperately want a friend. Most of the women in the car were still set on snubbing Francesca.

"Have you been there?" Molly asked, wide-eyed.

"A month or so ago," Francesca said, watching the car's rear door for any sign of that son of a bitch, Fargo. Well, she supposed he wasn't a complete son of a bitch, and went to graze a palm over her breast. She caught herself, though, looked pointedly at Molly, and said, "I just came from there. Paris is simply lovely this time of year."

That was, what she'd seen of it this time, which was mostly a fleeting glimpse or two from the hansom cab's window while she hurried from the train depot to the docks.

The rear door opened, and in stepped Fargo, along with several other men. She forced a smile onto her face and sent him a little wave. The bastard. He grinned back and began the claustrophobic job of fighting his way forward through the car toward her.

"Oh, my," said Molly, who seemed suitably impressed. Also, a little flustered. "He's so handsome! Is that your beau?" she whispered behind her hand. "Your husband?"

"Something like that, dear," Francesca said as Fargo neared. "Something like that."

"Thank God," said Korchenko, who was sweeping up the last of the broken glass from the large table lamp in the Pullman's parlor. The scattered books were picked up and back in the bookcase, but several of the pictures were hanging on the walls at odd angles. He hadn't got to those yet.

Probably waiting for me to fix them, Stacy thought, and snorted softly.

He was still angry, still incensed. To think that some range hand—some drifter, by God!—would speak to him in that manner, would simply take their money without a care to paying it back, was beyond words!

Fargo should have simply opened his shirt and asked to be stabbed, that's what he should have done. It was the gentlemanly thing to do. And the stinking saddle tramp still had their crown!

"I can't see how you can begin to think this is lucky, Vladimir," he said aloud. "Remember the moment we realized that we were not attached to the train any longer? Remember the way you shouted when we began to catch up with nothing to slow us but prayer? And even that was fruitless."

Stacy mopped at his brow. "The impact could have killed us. And we were very nearly abandoned in the wilderness! We could have been murdered by savage Indians or caught in a stampede of buffalo! We might have starved to death! Or frozen to death!"

" 'Nearly' is the key word, Franklin," said Korchenko, quite calmly, ignoring all of Stacy's "could have been" scenarios. He abandoned his sweeping and settled down in his chair.

Stacy sighed and picked up the little broom and dust bucket, but Korchenko held up a hand and waved it lazily. "Leave it, my dear Franklin. Let the porter tend to it in the morning. You have more important things to do tonight."

Stacy dropped the equipment and slumped into his chair, glass crunching under his shoes.

"Just let met kill him, Vladimir," he said, half pleading. "One sure sharp cut with the knife . . ."

Strangely, Korchenko smiled. "Fargo has made you very angry, has he not, Franklin?"

"Certainly, he has!"

The train hadn't built up much speed, and Stacy felt it slowing again. It ground slowly to a halt.

"I believe this is the infamous water stop," said Korchenko. He lit a cigar and puffed at it for a moment.

"I am pleased to see you so upset by this prairie varlet's cavalier attitude and demeanor," he continued. "But you must temper your passions for the time being, my dear Franklin. Later, there will be time enough for killing." He rolled off his excess ash in the crystal tray at his side. "For killing both of them."

Stacy didn't reply.

Suddenly, Korchenko looked at the wall above Stacy's head. "Dear me. Franklin, would you mind? Those crooked pictures will drive me mad."

15

"But I have to go," Bobby whispered, twitching. "Now!"

Fargo lay beside him, having been kicked out of the upper berth by a tight-lipped Francesca.

He tore his gaze away from the berth above long enough to glance over at the fidgeting Bobby.

Well, hell. It wasn't even midnight, likely too early for Stacy or Korchenko to show their ugly faces. Maybe they wouldn't show them at all tonight. Maybe they'd thrown in the cards. That would sure be a nice change, wouldn't it?

Not likely, though.

But he took pity on the kid.

"All right. Go ahead. But make it quick."

Bobby grunted gratefully and slipped out. Fargo could hear his bare feet slapping the floor as he ran down the car, to the privy.

He turned his attention once again to the roof of his berth. Francesca was up there, damn her. Up there smelling nice, up there looking great with all her hair loose around her shoulders and her skin all creamy and her eyes half-closed, up there hating his innards. Why did she have to be so pigheaded?

She was as smart as she was beautiful, he'd give her that. She'd figured out what was going on—that it was he who had set loose Korchenko and Stacy's Pullman, and that he had to know that she'd visited them that afternoon.

But what did she expect? She would've had to have known that he'd do something about it. Better to tinker with the train a little than to go shooting the place up. That's what he thought, anyhow.

He figured she should just have admitted defeat, taken it gracefully, and gotten on with the festivities. Got on with the lovemaking, to put it more bluntly. But no, she had to go and get all riled up.

Women.

He'd never understand them if he lived to be a hundred.

"Francesca?" he said, just loud enough for her to hear.

No answer.

He tried again, and still there was no reply.

He rapped his knuckles on the boards overhead.

An instant later, the curtains at his shoulder parted, and Francesca's head, beautiful even upside down, appeared in the opening.

"What!" she hissed. Her hair formed a tumbling red curtain, swinging with the train's movement.

He tried his biggest, most convincing smile. "Sweetheart," he began, all persuasion, "there's no sense in getting your knickers in a twist. I only—"

"You're ruining my life, Fargo," she hissed. "Don't you realize that?"

"I wasn't ruinin' anything an hour ago," he said, at his charming best.

"Yes, you were, you snake," she snapped. "I just didn't know about it, that was all."

From behind the safety of curtains, somebody from another berth shouted, "Quiet!"

"Honestly," Francesca whispered. "You men! You think that just because you're passable lovers, you can—"

"Passable?" Fargo said with a cocked brow.

"Oh, all right!" Francesca hissed indignantly. "You know what I mean. But damn and blast your hide, Fargo, you're killing me! I was set, set for life, and then you had to come along."

"Baby," Fargo said softly, "you were only set until the day that Stacy and Korchenko caught up with you. And they would have, eventually. You're not out of the woods, yet, you know."

"Bull hockey," she spat. "I would have lost them. Eventually."

"Don't be so sure," he whispered. "They would have found you. I never met a more determined son of a bitch than our old friend Stacy, and I've got a feeling Korchenko makes him look like a piker. And when they caught up to you, darlin', there wouldn't have been enough of you left to bury."

She didn't have an answer for that. She just gave a snort and pulled her head back. The curtains fell closed again.

And then opened abruptly.

"Go screw yourself, Fargo," she said, and then disappeared again.

"Well," Fargo muttered to himself. "Guess she told me."

The curtains opened again and he braced himself for another wash of vitriol from Francesca's tongue, but it was only Bobby, back from the washroom. Before he could sling a leg onto the berth, however, Francesca reached down for him.

"You're sleeping up here, Bobby, dear," she purred. "Mr. Fargo has a lot of thinking to do."

"About what?" Bobby asked as she pulled him up. Fargo ducked his bare and kicking feet as they levitated skyward.

"About chivalry," she said. "About poor, helpless impoverished woman on their own." Fargo heard her curtains rustle, then close with a sharp pull.

"Helpless, my ass," Fargo muttered in the dark.

"What's chivalry?" Bobby asked, his voice muted.

"Settle in, sweetheart," she said, "and I'll tell you all about it."

"Will you folks kindly shut the hell up?" came the anonymous heckler's voice from somewhere in the car.

"Drop dead," shouted Fargo, and with a snort, firmly crossed his arms over his chest.

At the rear of the rushing train, in the Pullman's parlor, Stacy was making ready.

Gloves? *Check.*

He pulled them on. They were the finest kid leather, reasonably warm and thin enough that he could feel the embossing of a coin through them.

Knife? *Check.*

He slid this into his right-hand vest pocket, where it would be handy.

Garrotte? *Check.*

This went into the opposite vest pocket, the one over his heart.

He patted his jacket pocket for the fourth time, feeling for a familiar outline. The little bottle of chloroform and the requisite rag were there, at the ready.

"It is almost time, Franklin," Korchenko said, and closed the lid of his watch case with an expensive-sounding click.

"Yes, Vladimir," Stacy replied patiently. "I know."

Stacy pulled his jacket collar close around his neck and rued the fact that they'd had to do all of this in such a hurry, had to be coupled the very last on the train. He didn't relish having to walk all the way forward.

"I'm ready," he said. "I suppose."

He made his way to the front of the car and put his hand on the door's latch.

"Franklin?"

He sighed, rolled his eyes heavenward, then turned. "What is it this time, Vladimir?"

"I hope you realize that you'll need to go over the cars."

Stacy cocked his head. "I beg your pardon?"

Korchenko pointed toward the ceiling. "You shall need to travel over the rooftops, my friend. To avoid detection by the railway personnel. This is understood, is it not?"

The temperature of Stacy's blood suddenly dropped twenty degrees. "But Vladimir!"

Korchenko was adamant, though. Stacy could tell by those folded arms, the set of his chin. "This must be done in secrecy," Korchenko said. "At all costs."

"Easy for you to say, Vladimir," Stacy rumbled in protest. "You won't be the one freezing to death out there, battered by an icy wind, slipping and sliding at a perilous height and a breakneck pace. Not to mention, in mortal danger of falling to a gruesome death with every step!"

"No," said Korchenko matter-of-factly, "that would be you." He checked his watch again. "You had best be on your way."

Stacy's initial fear had been fast overcome by anger, and he slipped outside without a word of reply. Although he thought, *Remind me to kill you when I get back, Vladimir,* as he huffed his way up the caboose's ladder to the slippery roof.

This time, he believed that he almost actually meant it.

Against the biting wind, he struggled precariously forward over car after car, nearly losing his balance at least twice on the roof of each car, but always catching himself in time. In turn, he let himself carefully down on the ladder, crossed to the platforms between cars, then took the next ladder gingerly upward, only to fight his way forward over the top of the next car.

By the time he reached the first-class car, he was exhausted. His chest hurt from both the trauma of battling the wind and the cold air he'd had to breathe in. He stood outside for a long moment and hung onto the flimsy railing for dear life, until he caught his breath, until his lungs stopped aching from the exertion.

Grudgingly, he told himself that this unfortunate expenditure of energy—not to mention his severe discomfort at it—had been necessary, and that it was now equally necessary to stop and recover a bit.

What he didn't tell himself was that it might have

been easier if he was a tad thinner, or a tad younger. Or even slightly in shape.

But he didn't wish to let himself inside, huffing and puffing and waking everyone from a sound sleep when they should be comfortably dead to the world. And dead to his snooping about.

At last his breathing leveled out somewhat, and he reached into his pocket and brought out the vial of chloroform. He tucked it down inside his glove with the neck protruding at his wrist. Then he brought out the clean, white rag and balled it in his gloved fist.

He opened the door.

He was met with a rush of warm, humid air that smelled a little too strongly of unpleasant body odors. Although the sounds of snores didn't entirely replace the noisy clack of wheels, they muted it. Softly, he crept forward, past the porter dozing before the car's pot-bellied stove, looking for the right berths, checking the numbers.

He stopped before the ones he sought, pondering his options. Upper or lower? It struck him that Fargo would have probably preferred the upper berth and let that dratted boy sleep below. Francesca would likely be with him if he knew her whorish type, he thought with distaste. She would be no problem, at least, not right away. In fact, she could help him search, once they put Fargo away.

He didn't need to kill her right off the bat. Not when she could be useful.

This pleased his sense of order—and his sense of workmanlike ethics—but not his sense of justice. According to that, she should have been the very first to go.

All in good time, he told himself. Idly, he wondered if he couldn't get away with simply chloroforming her and casting her off the side of the train. It seemed the easiest option.

Ah, well. Later. There was time enough to think about it.

Slowly, he eased the curtains back.

He was a very tall man, and so he could see right away that indeed, Francesca was there, and that she was sound asleep.

But she wasn't sleeping with Fargo. No, she had the blasted child with her.

Stacy's lips tightened with displeasure. He started to close the curtains again, but just then the boy's eyes popped open.

"Hey!" the child yelped. "Mr. Stacy!"

Much more quickly than anyone could have expected, himself included, Stacy pulled the cork from the chloroform bottle in his glove, hastily dampened the cloth, and clapped it over the thrashing boy's mouth and nose.

Bobby's struggles woke Francesca, even as he sagged under the drug's influence.

Now, Stacy had assumed, understandably, that Francesca would be on his side. That she might, perhaps, take the cloth from him and put the boy the rest of the way out herself.

But instead, the churlish wench took one look at his hand clasped over the boy's nose, pulled back her arm, and attempted to punch him squarely in the nose!

Quickly, Stacy ducked, and her fist slid off the side of his face. And as he did so, he moved the rag from the boy's face to hers, holding her down until she stopped fighting, until she stopped moving entirely.

Then, panting slightly, he went back to the groggily muttering Bobby, holding the sickly sweet rag over the boy's face until he, too, was completely in the arms of Morpheus.

Quickly, Stacy corked the little bottle of chloroform. In his haste he had left it open, and quite a bit had slopped out onto the berth's mattress as well as Francesca's nightclothes. He thought there was still enough for Fargo, though. He pulled Francesca's curtains, lest the fumes cloud his mind more than they already had.

He shook his head in an attempt to clear it, gave

his head a twist to the right, a twist to the left, and took a deep breath.

He had seen the satchels placed at the foot of her berth, and decided that this was a happy event, after all. Francesca's possessions could be sorted through at his leisure, once he was certain Fargo was put away. That was, provided the conductor didn't wake up and ask him what the hell he was doing. And provided another passenger didn't get up to use the convenience and ask him much the same thing.

Blast Vladimir, anyway! Why couldn't he do his own dirty work?

But despite that perilous trip he'd made over the car roofs, despite the ever-present danger of apprehension, Stacy was actually quite enjoying himself.

Not that he'd ever let on to Vladimir.

And now, he thought, rubbing his hands together, *for that thieving saddle tramp.*

Once again, he soaked the rag.

Groggily, Fargo roused from the fringes of sleep—and the start of a potentially very nice dream about a dance hall he'd once been to in Rock Creek, Colorado, and a certain yellow-haired girl that worked there—and became aware that Francesca was certainly thrashing around a lot up there.

Hope she doesn't knock that young 'un clear out of bed, he thought sleepily, with an eye to his ceiling, and started to roll over.

But at that moment—the moment he began to turn, the moment that Francesca stopped her restless kicking and lay suddenly quiet—he smelled something.

Something sweet.

Something . . . wrong.

He sat up, abruptly twisting toward the curtains and grabbing for his gun. And in that same moment, a hand from the outside threw the curtains open.

Franklin Stacy paused, the soaked rag in his hand, and stared at him.

Down the barrel of his gun, Fargo glared back.

16

Fargo moved fast and lunged toward Stacy, gun first.

But he hadn't figured on the fat man being quite so nimble. Stacy had dropped the rag and, with a blast of icy air, was out the back door before Fargo swung his feet to the floor.

Swearing under his breath, Fargo rapidly pulled on his boots, jammed the gun down the front of his britches—no time to put his rig on—and took off after him.

Only once he was out on the little platform and halfway up the ladder to the roof of the next car did he think about Francesca and Bobby.

He kept climbing, though.

He pulled himself up to the roof of the car. The wind, frigid and biting, hit him like a giant cold hand. He braced himself and, squinting, spotted Stacy on the roof of the next car down. The big man glanced back, then scuttled away, crablike.

Fargo scuttled after him.

Unlike Stacy, Fargo let the wind work for him, and he made better time than Stacy did. By the time Stacy had reached the end of his car slipping and sliding, Fargo had traveled the length of one roof, vaulted to Stacy's without bothering with the ladder, and was halfway to him.

He grabbed Stacy by the collar just before he reached the ladder.

Stacy swung around and blindly lashed out at him.

He made contact, though. Fargo took a crushing blow to the shoulder and went flying, nearly rolling off the car.

The man was like a bear—no finesse, but what strength!

"You son a bitch!" Fargo shouted. "I was tryin' to be nice!" But his words were lost in the wind. The wind beating at his back, he picked himself up and ran at Stacy, head down, intending to butt him down to the rooftop, down on his back.

Fargo ran square into him, his head punching Stacy's belly.

It had absolutely no effect. Fargo simply bounced off, and the impact sent him back several feet. He sat down hard, right at the shivering edge of the car's rooftop.

He slithered and slipped, one leg going all the way off, then both. He kicked the air wildly, searching for something, anything, to take at least part of his weight. He glanced down, then quickly looked away. The ground below was speeding by at a terrifying rate.

Just when he thought he'd go over the edge, he caught himself on the exhaust pipe for the car's pot-bellied stove. It burned his hand like a bastard, but he bit back the pain and began to haul himself up.

A split second later, there was an ominous creak. The pipe moved beneath Fargo's clutching fingers. He gave a last, desperate heave, and miraculously got one leg back up and was able to brace himself against the edge of the roof at the same moment that the pipe broke off in his hand, flush with the rooftop.

He swore under his breath and flung the hot pipe away. His fingers were halfway to his mouth when he looked up to see Stacy's enraged face and hear his bellow. He'd had barely enough time to move when the big man pulled a knife from his pocket and, un-mindful of his perch, charged the still prostrate Fargo.

But the progress a man makes when he throws himself into the wind just isn't the same as when the wind is pushing at his back. Fargo had time to quickly roll to the side, toward the center of the car and away from the edge. Right at the moment, all he was thinking about was getting as far away from that knife as possible.

And he succeeded. When Stacy missed him, he also lost his precarious balance. He went down, skidding over the car's roof, gloved hands losing the knife, his fingers frantically searching for a hold—any hold at all—desperately snatching at the place where the pipe used to be.

His legs slipped over the side, and he hung there for a moment, flailing madly, while Fargo tried to get to him. Just because a man was a thief and a Class-A son of a bitch, it didn't mean he deserved to die, did it? He managed to get a grip on one of Stacy's hands—or rather, Stacy managed to clamp onto one of Fargo's for dear life.

Fargo hauled on him with all his strength, planting his heels and elbows hard when he found purchase. The wind whistled past his cold-numbed ears and bit through his bucks, and it felt as if his shoulder would come free of its socket, but still he held on.

Stacy managed to get one of his legs back up, just barely, just the toe of one shoe, and Fargo watched through squinted, wind-burned eyes as Stacy attempted to gain some sort of foothold. It was no use, though. Stacy's shiny city shoes slipped every time.

"Pull yourself higher! Dig in with your knee!" Fargo shouted, even as he felt Stacy's glove begin to slip beneath his hand.

Stacy felt it, too. For the first time, he looked Fargo right in the eye. He moved his mouth in a *"Please!"* but the wind whipped the sound from his lips.

And then the glove gave way. Stacy's hand slipped from it as if it had been buttered, that fast and that slick. Soundlessly, he dropped over the side of the speeding train.

Fargo dropped down into the third-class car and pulled the emergency cord. He grabbed a sleepy-eyed porter and told him what had happened—well, a version of it, anyway—and then ran through the cars until he came to first class.

Francesca was awake and rubbing her head. And sitting down one level, on the edge of his berth.

"Bobby?" was the first word from his breathless lips.

The boy leaned down from the upper berth. "That Mr. Stacy, he come up here and did something to me and Miss Francesca," he said woozily. "Held a cloth over my face. Smelled funny. And I feel kinda sick to my stomach, Fargo."

Fargo let go a breath he didn't realize he'd been holding. Thank God they were both all right!

"It'll go away, Bobby," he said. "He chloroformed you, but you'll be all right, I promise." He got a whiff of the bedclothes and added, "You'd best sleep down here, buster."

"Don't know as how I want to be your partner anymore, Fargo," the boy grumbled as he climbed down into Fargo's arms, then slipped into the lower berth. He rolled away and pulled the covers up. "You've got too many people tryin' to murderate you . . . and everybody you're with!"

Fargo silently agreed with him, and sat next to Francesca.

With a screech and a hiss, the train came to a complete stop, and then started to back up. Here and there up and down the aisle, tousled heads poked out from between curtains.

"Figures it's your fault," said a man, and Fargo recognized his voice as belonging to their heckler, from earlier. "First it's a gay romp, then it's arguing, and now it's the train! Dad blast you, sir!" the heckler added in a grumble, then ducked back inside his berth and closed the curtains with a jerk.

Fargo put his arm around Francesca and gave her a squeeze. In reply, she groaned.

"You okay?" he said softly.

"I'm going to kill that idiot Stacy," she muttered, fingers to her temples, eyes closed.

"I've got a feeling you're too late," Fargo said, and she looked up.

"What?" she asked. And then she sat up straight. "You're not serious. Are you?"

Her expression was so intense that he couldn't tell whether she was happy or sad about the possibility, and so he just said, "That's why the train's backing up. To go look for him."

Her green eyes widened. "You threw him off the train?"

"Not exactly."

"Then how?"

Fargo shrugged. "He sort of . . . fell off." He opened his hand, and Stacy's glove, which he'd been clutching all this time, fell from it into Francesca's lap.

Gingerly, she picked it up. Staring at it, she said, "I'd venture he made quite a splat."

All at once, Fargo relaxed. "Reckon he did," he said.

Franklin Stacy floated back to consciousness.

The first thing he was aware of was the pain, a sharp, biting pain in his leg and his arm, and the feeling that he'd been trampled by a herd of wild buffalo. Then, slowly he remembered what had just happened.

That blasted Fargo, damn him!

The desperate fight on the train's roof.

The abject terror when he lost his grip.

And falling, falling.

And then he realized that he was alone, all alone, in the middle of nowhere.

And that he was wet.

And that he was freezing cold.

He had landed in some sort of boggy marsh, landed flat on his back. It was a miracle he hadn't broken it. Or had he?

Carefully, he moved his fingers, then his toes. Both movements were accompanied by a great wash of pain, but at least he could still move them.

And it was quiet, incredibly quiet.

He was a man used to the constant clamor of city sounds: the clack of buggies and drays, shouts and crowds, and hustle and bustle. The silence frightened him as much as his pain.

The freezing mud he had landed in surrounded him, welling thickly between his legs and up his sides, and he made a tentative move to sit up. But the suction of the mud, combined with the sharp pain in his limbs (and the duller pains from every other point of his anatomy) convinced him otherwise.

"I shall die out here," he whispered dismally from a prone position. "Alone, alone, I'm all alone."

And then he began to weep. Never again would he see Vladimir, never again be comforted by all that he provided. But then, it was Vladimir who had sent him to his death, wasn't it?

The fiend.

Heartless fiend, to so ill-use him!

And all for that stupid crown.

"My life should have meant more," he said as he silently wept. He was going to die on the blasted prairie, in a Kansas bog.

His body would probably never be discovered, and he was going to die dirty—filthy dirty—and cold. He only prayed he would perish from his wounds before some wild animal discovered him as an easy meal.

But then, quite suddenly, he thought he heard something. He held his breath.

Yes, there it was! Something suspiciously akin to a train. And it was getting closer.

His train?

Had someone seen him fall? Surely, Fargo wouldn't have reported it. Why, Fargo had practically hurled him from the rocketing conveyance! He should be horse-whipped, flogged, tarred and feathered, then thrown from a train, himself. And when they found what was left of him, he should be drawn and quartered.

The train blew its whistle, a long screech into the night.

Would they spot him, Stacy wondered, if it was, indeed, him they were searching for? The train seemed to be approaching terribly slowly, and it was coming from the south. That was the direction they'd been heading.

He told himself that another train couldn't possibly have been switched onto the tracks this quickly, much less in the exact center of nowhere. It had to be his train. Didn't it?

But then, how long had he been unconscious? Why, it might have been twenty-four hours!

Panic set in again, but he suddenly realized that if he'd been dead to the world for that long, his stomach surely would have been growling quite angrily. And it was not.

No, he thought with a small sigh of relief, he'd only been unconscious for a few moments.

But how would they spot him in all this grass? He seemed to be surrounded by some sort of tall, reedy growth, about four-feet high and very thick. He supposed it was this tall grass and the mud—and his fat, of course, his glorious fat—that had kept him from shattering every bone in his body when he fell.

But now the reeds were going to shield him from his rescuers.

Once again, he tried to sit up.

This time he had more success, huffing out angry clouds of steam and bracing himself with the elbow of his good arm. The weeds were still high over his head, though, and the sound of the approaching train grew steadily nearer and nearer.

In desperation, he gave his enormous body a giant heave forward, and stopped in a sitting position, his hand replacing his elbow as a prop.

But his leg, oh, his leg!

If it had burnt like a brand before, it was now surely suffering the torments of Hell, and he along with it.

"Damn!" he hissed through clenched teeth, just before he passed out again.

17

Stacy awoke back inside the Pullman, on Korchenko's soft bed, with a man he assumed to be a doctor shaking his head and *"tut-tutting"* beside him. He moved slightly, and the doctor brightened visibly.

"Well!" he said. "Your friend is awake, Mr. Korchenko."

Korchenko's worried face suddenly leaned into the periphery of his vision, and he turned toward it.

"Vladimir," said Stacy. His tongue felt incredibly thick in his mouth.

"Franklin," said Korchenko, and took his hand. He flicked his fingertips toward the doctor. "Leave us," he commanded.

"Be outside," the doctor said. "Holler if you need me." He slipped out the door.

Korchenko sat on the edge of the bed just as Stacy realized that someone had cleaned him up. His muddy suit was gone, he was wearing his dressing gown, and his broken leg and arm were heavy with makeshift splints.

He felt rather warm and wonderful, too.

"Did they give me laudanum, Vladimir?" he asked Korchenko.

Korchenko ignored the question. "Did you find it, Franklin?"

Stacy blinked. He didn't know whether his bravery came from the laudanum or from his close brush with death, but he said, "The crown? And no questions as to what in the world happened to me at that villain's hands? No query as to the state of my health?" He shook his head. "I must say, Vladimir, I heartily disapprove of your attitude."

Korchenko threw down the hand he'd been holding. Haughtily, he snapped, "And I heartily disapprove of yours, Franklin. You were saved, by God. That is all that should concern *you,* I suppose, but I have other fish, much larger fish, to gut and fry. Now, where is my crown?"

Disheartened, his leg starting to thump once more, Stacy explained what had happened. It wasn't fair that Vladimir should treat him this way, he thought. It wasn't fair at all. After all the plots he had contrived, the excuses he had made, the webs he had woven—and become entangled in, himself—and the people he had killed for Vladimir, he deserved better treatment.

But nothing was ever good enough for Vladimir, now, was it?

Still, old habits died hard. When he finished his recitation, he waited, like a dog, to be beaten or praised. Metaphorically speaking, of course.

But all Korchenko did was press his fingers to his temples and turn away.

"What?" demanded Stacy. "You have nothing to say to me?"

Korchenko turned toward him. "Only that you disappoint me, Franklin. You have disappointed me very greatly."

Strangely, Stacy was relieved. The lash of Korchenko's tongue again. Blessed familiarity.

"I can see that I shall have to take matters into my own hands," Korchenko went on. "We have only four hours before this train reaches Kansas City, at which point our thieving friend, Fargo, will be at liberty to go in any direction, by any conveyance. Including overland on horseback. I do not believe you are up to chasing him, Franklin."

Stacy wanted to say that neither of them were, but held his tongue.

"Well," said Korchenko, standing erect. "I shall send the doctor back in. Shall I?"

He didn't wait for a reply. He simply rattled out the door, to be replaced by the doctor.

"How you doin'?" the doctor asked, then held out his hand. "Groom," he said. "Heber Groom. I'm a veterinarian down to Kansas City, goin' home right now. Guess I was the closest thing they could find to a doctor on this train."

Stacy groaned.

Heber Groom, DVM, perched on the edge of the bed, grinning wide. Likely, he was happy to at last have a patient who could talk back to him.

"Course, busted bones is busted bones, whether they belong to horse, dog, sheep, or man," he went on. "That's right, isn't it?" He paused to pat Stacy's shoulder. "Don't think you've got any internal injuries. Least, you're not shittin' any blood. Say, you need another hit of that joy juice, there? You're lookin' a tad green around the gills."

Stacy simply pursed his lips and closed his eyes.

Oh, the indignity!

Fargo lay in the cramped lower berth, squeezed like a sardine in a tin with Francesca and Bobby. At least the two of them seemed to be getting along famously. Bobby was curled in Francesca's arms, his drowsing head on her shoulder. She had fallen asleep with her fingers laid gently on the child's temple.

They made quite a pair. Both were as tough on the outside as they were all soft and gooey on the inside, and neither of them would admit it. For the first time, it came to Fargo that maybe they belonged together. After all, they were both on their own, weren't they? He had the distinct feeling that Bobby's "uncle" in California was just an excuse to get there.

Of course, Francesca would never take on a child, even if one was left on her doorstep, so to speak. It would cramp her style, slow her down, trip her up.

He reached for his watch and discovered that he

could barely move his arms, trapped as they were on one side by Bobby and the other by the bed curtains.

Well, the spilled chloroform would have most likely evaporated by this time, he supposed. He'd moved up top and try to catch a few hours of shut-eye before they hit Kansas City.

Finally—and wondering how he'd ever gotten in here in the first place—he managed to open the curtains. He very nearly fell on the floor without their brace and caught himself with one hand. Then he closed them behind him and climbed to the upper berth, where he gratefully stretched out.

He hadn't pulled the curtains yet, and he checked his pocket watch in the light coming from the aisle.

A little better than three hours, he figured. He also didn't figure that Korchenko would try anything alone. He hadn't so far, anyway.

And according to the conductor, Stacy was very much alive, if suffering from a dunking in the mud, a lot of bruises, and a broken leg, arm, and collarbone. He wouldn't be up and around for a good long time.

Still, something gnawed at the back of Fargo's mind. He wouldn't be able to get a good night's sleep until he hit Kansas City and got the damned Moldavian Crown off his hands and into those of a federal agent.

He wondered if anybody was in Kansas City yet—anybody with any authority, that was. He'd wired Washington from the hotel in Lincoln, wired an old friend of his in the State Department, Henry Stroud. He hoped Henry was in his office when the wire came. He hoped that he'd contacted somebody out here. Somebody good.

He didn't want the responsibility of that doodad any longer than he had to bear up under it, but he sure wasn't going to turn it over to some addlepated, bureaucratic tinhorn who'd only get it stolen again.

His hand hadn't been as badly burned as he feared. It was only a little red, but Francesca had covered it in some sort of goop from her handbag and wrapped it in a clean white cloth.

He studied it in the dim light, and pressed his palm with a finger. It didn't even hurt anymore. Either he was a whole lot faster a healer than he remembered, or that unguent of hers had worked miracles.

He was dead tired. Running across the tops of trains did that to a fellow, he thought with a brief smile. He supposed he really ought to stay awake, just in case Korchenko tried something, but he was so damned tired! Of course, if there hadn't been anything to do, anything to be alert for, he would have tossed and turned and not got a wink. His mind would have raced the whole night through.

Wasn't that always the way? When you had to stay awake because of something or other—for instance, potential chloroform-carrying thieves creeping up on you—that's when your eyelids felt the heaviest and your body the most grateful to be lying down.

Damned if you do, damned if you don't.

Fargo put his gun under his pillow and tried to stay awake.

He woke with a jerk.

He didn't know what time it was, but it was still dark. And somebody was rustling about, out in the aisle.

I hope it's that moron, the heckler, he thought. *This time, I'll give him a piece of* my *mind.*

He reached to pull the curtains, but somebody beat him to it.

Korchenko.

At least, he assumed it was Korchenko. Mostly because he had the struggling boy tucked under one arm, and he was pointing a gun at Fargo.

"Give me my property," he hissed.

"Let the boy go," Fargo said. He was at a distinct disadvantage. He was lying down, for one thing, and Korchenko's line of vision was such that if he went for the gun under his pillow, he'd be dead before he reached it.

He must have flicked his eyes toward it unconsciously, because Korchenko said, "Ah, a concealed weapon? Go ahead. I am a desperate man, Mr. Fargo. If I have to kill every man, woman, and child in this car, I will do so."

Fargo believed him. His eyes were slitted with intensity, his voice persuasive and foreign beneath the threat. Fargo figured that he couldn't really kill everybody on the car, not before somebody took him out, but he did believe that Korchenko would give it a sincere try.

Slowly, he raised his hand. "Easy," he said. "Just whoa up."

"Better," said Korchenko.

Bobby made another fruitless effort to escape his clutches, and this time Korchenko simply popped the boy over the head with the butt of his gun.

It was so quick—and unexpected—that Fargo had no time to react. By the time he even thought about going for his pistol, Korchenko was holding a limp Bobby under his arm, and his gun was right back where it had been, pointed square at Fargo's face.

"The Moldavian crown, if you please, Mr. Fargo?" Korchenko said again. "I am growing impatient."

"Is Francesca all right?" Fargo asked, stalling for time.

"For the moment," Korchenko replied, his voice clipped. "The crown, sir."

"All right, all right," Fargo said resignedly. "I've gotta come down." He moved his legs, intending to swing them over the side of the berth. And square into Korchenko's head.

But Korchenko was too clever. Quickly, he stepped back, away from Fargo's poised legs, and said, "Tut, tut, Mr. Fargo. Slowly, please."

Teeth gritted, Fargo eased his legs over the side of the bed, then dropped to the floor. He knew there was no way in hell that Korchenko would allow either him or Francesca to live once he had his bauble. He'd have to take a chance on handing it over. Maybe Korchenko would have a moment of weakness, be distracted by its glitter just long enough to give Fargo an opening.

After all, Korchenko wasn't that big, and he sure didn't weigh much. And he had at least twenty years on Fargo. He told himself that he might just be able to pull it off.

Fargo put his hand on Francesca's curtains.

"Your permission?" he asked.

Korchenko answered with a curt yet civilized nod. "Just don't attempt anything unwise," he said almost amicably, and beneath his arm, jostled the unconscious boy's body.

Fargo pulled back the curtains.

Francesca was there, all right, and she was fine, except for being bound hand and foot and gagged. She rolled her eyes from Fargo to Korchenko and lingered on Bobby before she looked at Fargo again. Her eyes were pleading, frightened.

Fargo whispered, "It'll be all right," even though he wasn't sure of any such thing, and reached down to the foot of the bed. He pulled his hat out from beneath the jumble of their possessions.

He stood erect, the hat in his hands. "Here," he said.

Korchenko shot him a puzzled look.

"It's in here," Fargo said, holding it out. "Go ahead. Take it."

From the periphery of his vision, Fargo saw Francesca roll her eyes in belated revelation.

Korchenko caught on at the exact same moment. "The inner hatband," he said. "Clever, Mr. Fargo." He wiggled the nose of his gun. "Produce it, if you please."

Fargo turned the hat upside down and stuck his fingers beneath the inner hat band.

Nothing.

He peered closer, and turned the whole of the inner band inside out.

The crown was gone.

145

18

"Enough," said Korchenko, and this time he didn't sound so amiable. "The crown. Now."

Numbly, Fargo held the hat out toward him. "It was in here," he said, still flabbergasted. "I swear it!"

Korchenko cocked his gun's hammer. "Enough!" he barked.

"Will you goddamn people shut the hell up?" came a new voice. The heckler's.

Korchenko's eyes flicked toward the sound. Fargo's hand shot out and up before the heckler had completed his complaint.

He knocked Korchenko's arm away. Korchenko fired, but the bullet hit nothing but air. The gun sailed from Korchenko's fingers, skidding down the aisle and lodging under one of the berths. By that time, Fargo had thrown himself forward and down, pinning Korchenko—and Bobby—on the floor of the narrow aisle.

For an older man, the son of a bitch fought like a tiger. Worse, the unconscious Bobby was between them, and Korchenko landed a couple of jarring, bony punches to Fargo's midsection while Fargo was still having to pull his on account of the boy.

Korchenko had just landed a good right-hand jab to the side of his head when a half-dazed Fargo finally got Bobby mostly out of the way and clipped Korchenko hard on the chin.

Korchenko let out an indignant roar and, adrenaline

flowing, somehow managed to flip Fargo completely over his head.

Fargo landed on his back with a surprised *"Oof!"*

But he wasn't too surprised to reach overhead and punch straight down with his fist, hitting Korchenko in the nose. There was a satisfying crunch of cartilage and bone.

Fargo didn't stop to appreciate it, though. Quick as a cat, he rolled over and jumped to his feet. Korchenko was on his knees by that time, blood streaming from his nose.

Fargo aimed a kick that was meant to catch Korchenko under the chin, but Korchenko threw himself forward before Fargo could connect. He butted Fargo in the belly, and Fargo flew backward a few feet at an angle, his back connecting with the hard rail of an upper berth.

"That hurts, goddamn it!" he shouted, as the female occupant of the berth shrieked and pulled her head back inside.

Up the entirety of the car, stunned, bewildered, and frightened faces protruded from curtains like the heads of so many turtles from their shells.

"I intended that it should hurt," panted Korchenko, and wiped the blood from his nose on his expensive sleeve. "And I intend that this should cause you even more pain."

A gentleman's blade—narrow and about four inches long—suddenly jacked down into his hand.

"Shall we dance, Mr. Fargo?" he asked, his skeleton's face curled into a parody of a smile.

"Sorry, Korchenko," Fargo replied, gulping for air. What he wouldn't give for a gun! And his back smarted something fierce. He ignored the pain. "My dance card's full," he snarled.

Korchenko lunged for him.

Fargo jumped back again, but a moving train wasn't exactly the best arena for a fight, and this time he caught his heel on the fancy wrought-iron base of a berth.

He went down again, spraddle-legged.

Grinning evilly, Korchenko leapt on top of him, blade poised.

But not before Fargo's searching fingers met the butt of Korchenko's gun, which had been knocked under the berth that had tripped him.

He snatched it up, his fingers righting it out of long habit, and he swung his arm free.

His shot took Korchenko in the chest.

Korchenko fell, blade first. Fargo stuck up his left arm in the nick of time, catching the man's body and rolling it to the side. The blade's tip left a jagged mark across the front of his buckskin shirt, but didn't cut through it.

He lay there for a moment, panting, with Korchenko's corpse half-on, half-off him. The slug had taken the thin man through the heart, and he had died instantly.

And the car was quiet. You could have heard a pin drop in there, if it hadn't been for the incessant background noise of iron wheels on iron rails.

But then, just when Fargo was thinking about getting Korchenko off of him and standing up, the passengers began to applaud. It started out with one pair of clapping hands—belonging to a stranger—and then another pair joined in, and pretty soon the entire car was filled with hoots and whistles.

A porter came from somewhere and helped him with Korchenko while night-shirted passengers leaned from their berths to pat him on the back or shake his hand. Bobby, who had been snatched out of harm's way by an elderly woman in a bottom berth, released himself from her protective arms to run to Fargo.

"Wow!" he cried over the hubbub. "That was some fight!"

Fargo felt the boy's head and found a knot. "Looks like you've got a real turkey egg there, kid," he said, and grinned.

"Aw, I've had me worse," said Bobby, trying to shrug it off.

"And thank you, ma'am," Fargo said to the woman who had rescued the boy.

"My pleasure, sir," she replied primly. "Any man who would use a child in the way that he did," she added, indicating the late Mr. Korchenko, who was being carried from the car by the porter and another passenger, "ought to be horsewhipped. Or worse."

"Yes, ma'am," Fargo said, thinking that he had, indeed, given Korchenko far worse.

The car was quieting down again, and Fargo heard a muffled, *"Mmm! Mmm, mmm, mmm!"* behind him. Francesca!

With Bobby, he went to her and removed her gag, then her ropes.

"About bloody time," she muttered, rubbing her wrists. "And where is it, really?" she added, picking up his hat and tossing it at him. "The crown."

He boosted Bobby up to the upper berth.

"Oh, come on," he said, sitting next to her. "You've got it and you know it. Don't try to horseshit me."

Her mouth opened and closed again indignantly. "I have no such thing! Search me all you want, you dirty-dealing, no-account, crown-thieving—"

He kissed her, if for nothing more than to just shut her up. And behind him, the car erupted once again into cheers and whistles.

Grinning against her lips, he pulled the curtains closed around them.

When they pulled into Kansas City a few hours later, Fargo was tired but happy, and Francesca seemed sated, if a little weary. And she at last had been convinced that he no longer had the crown.

Well, as convinced as he could make her.

Bobby, on the other hand, was bright and excited. He'd never been to Kansas City.

They were met by one Archibald P. Longworthy, in the employ of the United States government, who got on the train while they were still collecting their things, and while the porters were still tending to putting up the berths.

"Would have known you anywhere, Mr. Fargo," Longworthy was saying. He was a medium-sized man, probably forty, and very average looking. "Henry Stroud described you to a *T*. And of course," he confided, "I've read all your books."

"Don't believe everything you read," said Fargo without expression. "And I didn't write 'em. I'm just the unfortunate subject."

"Well," said Longworthy, bringing his briefcase up and resting it on the rumpled sheets of a lower berth, "it was fortunate that I just happened to be in Kansas City. Very fortunate, indeed. I understand that you have something for me?"

He unsnapped his briefcase and pulled a smallish box from its interior, then opened it. It was lined in blue velvet, but otherwise empty.

"If you please, Mr. Fargo?"

Fargo just stared at him. And Longworthy, misunderstanding, said, "Oh dear. I supposed you'll need to see my papers first. Quite remiss of me." He began to search through his briefcase.

Fargo said, "It doesn't matter. See, I—"

Bobby tugged at his pant leg.

"What, kid?" Fargo asked a little impatiently. "Can't you see I'm talking to somebody?"

"Yeah, I see," Bobby said, and reached up to fish beneath the upper berth's mattress. "Just thought you might want this."

He produced the Moldavian Crown. It glittered and gleamed in the early morning sun forcing its way through the windows. Fifty perfect diamonds sparkled, four large, flawless rubies gave off fiery sparks, and a scattered handful of Kashmir sapphires shown like solid bits of deep ocean water, all in a filigreed tiara of burnished gold, slightly bent out of shape.

"Holy crud," said a man across the aisle, and blinked.

"Indeed," said Francesca, who was right behind Fargo, having just come back from the washroom.

Bobby grinned.

"Remind me to take you to the woodshed, you little monkey," whispered Fargo, and the boy's grin broadened.

Fargo and Bobby walked slowly down the station's platform. He had fully expected Francesca to stay over for at least the night, but she had said no, she was off to Lincoln again, now that he'd ruined her life, stolen her future, and killed off her chances of doing anything but going to work for Mae.

He was sorry that she had to feel that way, sorry that her vision was so narrow, although he had, fruitlessly, tried talking her out of it. If she hadn't decided early on to be a thief, she could have been quite a lady.

Come to think of it, she was quite a gal anyhow.

"So, how'd you figure out that the crown was in my hat?" he asked Bobby.

"Well," the boy said indignantly, "you didn't have no place else to keep it. I knew it wasn't in your satchel. And I noticed that you didn't wear it when you had to do anything stealthy. And besides," he added, suddenly smug, "that's where I would'a put it."

Fargo put at hand on the boy's shoulder, and they stopped to watch while the sheriff and a couple of deputies removed Stacy from the Pullman. They had the help of a few porters, who struggled under the weight of Stacy's stretcher.

Stacy didn't spot him, being drugged to the gills, and Fargo made no attempt to catch his eye.

Korchenko's body was blanketed on a bench on the platform.

"Get the live ones first," muttered Fargo.

"Huh?" said Bobby.

"Nothing," said Fargo, and they began to walk again.

"How come the sheriff didn't arrest Miss Francesca?" the boy asked.

"Because she didn't do anything wrong. At least, not in this country."

"But she stole the—"

"Yeah," cut in Fargo, "but she stole it in Europe. I don't understand all the legalities of these things, Bobby. I just do what I'm told, and this time I was told by Mr. Longworthy of the State Department. All official-like." He smiled at the boy. "You feel like some breakfast?"

"I could eat me a bear and a plum puddin' after!" Bobby said with enthusiasm.

"I'll just bet you could," said Fargo with chuckle.

They had no more than stepped down off the platform to the dusty street when a new fellow, his clothes and demeanor completely out of place in Kansas City, hurried up to them. He was small of stature, badly bruised behind his glasses—one lens of which was missing—and wearing a rumpled dark gray suit and a bowler hat.

"The sheriff! I need the sheriff!" he cried.

"You sure look like it, buddy," Fargo said. He jabbed a thumb back toward the platform. "He's back there, with the stretcher."

The man had no more scurried on by them than Fargo stopped dead in his tracks.

"Shit!" he hissed, and yanking Bobby behind him, quickly followed in the little man's wake.

"What's 'a matter?" hollered Bobby.

Fargo didn't answer.

They caught up to the small man just as he was gesturing wildly at the sheriff, who so far had done nothing but tell him to slow the hell down, dammit. Behind him, porters and deputies rolled their eyes at the delay. They were carrying Stacy's stretcher, after all, and he wasn't light.

Fargo grabbed the little man by the shoulder and wheeled him around. "What's your name?" he asked.

"L-Longworthy," the man stuttered. "Archibald P. Longworthy. And take your hands off me, sir! I have been battered about enough, of late!"

"Prove it," growled Fargo.

The man looked at Fargo as if he were out of his

mind. "Why, look at my face, sir! Both eyes blackened, and I just got free of those blasted ropes. The blackguards broke my glasses, and I believe they broke my nose! Nothing but thugs and rogues west of the Mississippi!"

"I don't mean prove you were beat up, you dunce," Fargo shouted. "Prove you're Longworthy!"

The man snorted and abruptly turned back toward the sheriff.

But Fargo wheeled him around again before he could more than open his mouth. "State Department?" he asked.

Longworthy started in surprise, then said, "Yes. Why?"

At this point, the fat man on the stretcher roused, pointed a finger at Fargo, and said groggily, "You, sir!" before he dropped back in a faint.

He was ignored by everyone.

"You a friend of Henry Stroud?"

Longworthy tipped his bruised face. "I've known Henry for years, if it's any of your business. And who might you be, if I may be so bold?"

Fargo swore under his breath, and then said, "The man who's gonna get you that crown."

The little man seemed to prick up his ears at that. "What? What do you know about the crown?" Longworthy—the real Longworthy—shouted as Fargo sprinted down the platform.

"Who was that man? Exactly what in the world is going on?" Longworthy asked Bobby as they, along with the sheriff, watched Fargo run down the length of the platform and leap toward the waiting train.

"Kinda complicated," said the boy, and shrugged. "You got a few minutes, mister?"

19

They were just sitting there, as bold as brass: Francesca and the phony Longworthy. Just sitting there, laughing quietly about something or other—him, probably—and waiting for the train to pull out.

Their backs were to him, and Fargo stood there a moment, letting the boarding passengers jostle him from behind. When the hell had she wired ahead? Where had this compatriot come from, anyway?

There were several stops where she could have stepped off and sent a wire, he supposed. For the first few legs of the ride, the train had practically stopped at people's farms to pick them up. But how the hell had she known to wire anybody at all? How in the world had she known about Henry Stroud?

And then he realized that she didn't have to know, not about Henry. All she had to know, from something that he or the boy had said or inferred, was that he had sent a wire from Lincoln. This man had stolen Longworthy's briefcase, and there was likely something in there with Henry's name on it.

That, or the real Longworthy had mentioned Stroud's name, and his relationship to Fargo.

It didn't matter. Francesca was as smart as a whip, and she was single-minded. He had known that. He should have been mindful of it. He should have made Bobby mindful of it.

Well, now it was indelibly etched in his mind.

It didn't matter who this son of a bitch was, or how

he'd sniffed out the real Longworthy and replaced him. What did matter was that he and Francesca thought they had made off with the crown once and for all, thought they'd outfoxed him.

They were wrong.

He moved forward, drawing his sidearm as he walked, and jabbed its cold nose into the back of the neck of the fake Longworthy. Longworthy froze mid-chuckle.

Francesca looked up, and the smile fell from her face.

"Goddamn it," she said with a disgusted sigh. "Won't you ever go away?"

"Nice to see you, too," Fargo replied.

From the seat behind the false Longworthy, a drummer said, "See here, sir! I don't believe firearms are—"

"Shut the hell up and mind your own business," Fargo snapped.

"Well, I never!" said the gent. "Conductor!"

Fargo ignored him. "Bring it up," he said to Francesca, and nodded toward the briefcase. "Nice and easy."

Reluctantly, she eased the briefcase up from the floor.

"Open it," Fargo said.

She didn't.

"Honey, if you don't open that thing, I'm gonna spatter your boyfriend's brains all over these nice people," he said. "Don't think I won't. I don't know him from Adam."

She folded her arms and glared at him.

The man behind them yelled, "Conductor!" again.

Fargo cocked his gun.

The false Longworthy, Fargo's gun still at his neck, hissed, "Francesca! Please!"

She closed her eyes and pursed her pretty lips. "Oh, all right!" she spat. She opened it.

"Now take out the case."

She did.

"Open that, too."

She did.

There was the crown, safe and secure. Well, almost. It wouldn't be safe until he put it in the hands of the real Longworthy. Probably wouldn't be safe even then, but at least his hands would be washed of it.

"About time!" grumbled the man behind them. "You see? You see what's going on? We're being robbed at gunpoint!"

From behind, the conductor's hand tentatively closed on Fargo's gun arm. Without looking, Fargo hauled off and punched the owner of the encroaching hand in the face. The hand fell away.

"All right," Fargo said, his attention on Francesca and her compatriot. "Close everything up and hand it over."

"Dear God!" hissed the passenger behind them. Fargo heard a thunk as the man pushed the unconscious conductor off his lap.

Francesca closed the cases, all right, but she stalled out at the handing-it-over part.

"Francesca . . ." Fargo began.

"Oh, take it," she said suddenly, thrusting the case across her companion's lap. "Happy now? I suppose the sheriff is right behind you. I won't look pretty in prison drabs, I can assure you."

Fargo picked up the briefcase and clamped it under his arm. "Call me soft, Francesca," he said, "but I'm not doing anything except getting off this train. You were sure a challenge. Don't think I've ever met anybody quite like you."

Faintly, he heard the head conductor calling, "All aboard!" and heard the hiss of steam. The train gave a little jolt and started to crawl along.

Francesca smiled at him, her most enticing smile. She said, "Fargo, honey, wouldn't you consider—?"

"No," he said, stepped over the woozy conductor, and backed down the aisle. The man behind him had frozen in his seat, hands in the air. Once the gun was away from his neck, Francesca's companion immediately ducked his head. But Francesca just sat there, twisted in her seat, glaring at him.

Or rather, the briefcase.

He reached the back door of the compartment, and opened it. "See you around," he called.

"Not if I can help it," she called back with what he thought was a hint of a smile.

And then he stepped outside and hopped off the train, briefcase in hand.

He holstered his gun, gave his head a puzzled shake as the train went past him to leave the station. And then, briefcase in hand, he started back down the long platform, toward the sheriff, Bobby, and Longworthy.

He was whistling.

"So, what you gonna do about the kid?" Rose asked. She lay in his arms naked, a fine skin of sweat dewing her face and body. After a long bout of love-making, they were both sweating and tired, but happily so. At least he didn't have to worry about her ransacking his possessions while he was asleep.

Good old Rose.

"I sent a wire," he said, reaching for the champagne bottle. There was just one warm swig left, and he took it. "Turns out that uncle of his was for real, after all. Mr. Coats of Sacramento," he said, making a swirl in the air with the bottle. He reached over the side of the bed, put the bottle down, and felt around for his britches.

"You hear back?" Rose asked, snuggling closer.

"Yup." He pulled a hastily folded piece of paper from his pocket and smoothed it on his knee, then showed it to her. He already knew what it said:

MARTHA AND JUNIOR SEND LOVE STOP SEND BOBBY STOP OUR HOME IS HIS STOP S COATS

Rose read it, then handed it back. "Sounds like a ready-made family. Brother and everything." She smiled. "Lucky kid."

"Yeah, he is," Fargo said. Especially lucky, since he was stuffing his face with cakes and cookies and Indian fry bread right at that moment, in the care of a couple of the girls from downstairs. It was late afternoon and they weren't any too busy. And besides, they liked to have a kid to fuss over.

Come to think of it, Bobby might not want to leave!

"When you sendin' him?" Rose asked. She kissed the point of his shoulder.

"Oh, reckon I'll ride him out," Fargo replied. "Want to make sure he's settled in and happy. And I want to meet this uncle of his for myself."

"You really like that boy, don't you?"

He gave her a little hug. "Reckon I do, Rosie. Yessir, reckon I do."

Stacy was in jail, Korchenko was dead, Francesca—bless her larcenous heart—was on her way to who-knew-where. The Ovaro was in a fine fettle, and he and Bobby were about to set off on an adventure, the kind that any boy would remember for a lifetime. And Fargo had Rose.

It had been a pretty good couple of days.

He hugged Rose close, then cupped one of her breasts with his hand and dipped his head to kiss it.

She grinned. "Again, Fargo, you old dog?"

"Again, Rosie."

"Come to Mama, sugar."

Six months later, after Bobby was delivered to his uncle—who turned out to be quite a nice fellow—and Fargo was up in Montana, a small, battered package arrived for him.

It was stickered and stamped with a dozen addresses, and looked to have been following him all over the West. But the return address was Washington, D.C., and the sender was Henry Stroud at the State Department.

Fargo sat down on a barrel in front of the dry goods store and tore off the string, then the paper. Beneath, he found a small, black velvet box and a letter. He opened the letter first.

Hello you old jackass!
I trust you're alive and well. Doesn't seem like God wants you to die yet, although you certainly keep testing His patience. I enclose a small gift from Their Royal Highnesses, the King and Queen of Moldavia. They were tick-led pink to get their bauble back, and they awarded you with the Moldavian Cross. Also, a tidy sum of money, herein also enclosed.

Fargo opened the letter all the way, and a small stack of bills fluttered to the sidewalk. He scooped them up and made a quick count. Two thousand, all in hundred dollar bills.

Now, this was the kind of letter he didn't mind trudging to the post office for!

He tucked the bills into his pocket, and returned to the letter.

Guess they don't have a clue to what a rascal you really are. Take care. My longstanding offer of a job still holds, if you ever want to stop playing hero to the masses and settle down.

Regards, Henry

Smiling, Fargo folded the letter and stuck that into his pocket, too.

Then he opened the black velvet box.

Inside was a real crackerjack of a gold medal, rib-boned in green, yellow, and white. It was scribbled all around in a language he couldn't understand, and in its center was what he was pretty sure was a small ruby.

"I'll be damned," he said softly. "I'll just be dou-ble damned."

"Hey, Fargo!" called an excited voice from across the street. Bill Sykes, a local stuck in a mess of trouble with a gang of roughnecks, had just ridden up with the Ovaro alongside of him. "We gonna get this posse put together or what?"

"Right with you, Bill," Fargo answered. He jammed the box and its medal into his pocket as he crossed the street. Then he leapt up on the Ovaro and reined him around. "Let's get to it," he said.

"Ye-ha!" Bill yelped, fanning the air with his hat.

And with that, the two men galloped down the street and over the hills.

LOOKING FORWARD!

**The following is the opening
section from the next novel in the exciting
Trailsman series from Signet:**

THE TRAILSMAN #253
DEAD MAN'S HAND

*Oregon Territory, 1861—
In some casinos you lose not only your money
but your life—something the Trailsman aims
to put a stop to.*

Skye Fargo was not surprised to hear gunfire. He was
well aware of Cumberland, Oregon's, reputation as a
hell town and haven for gamblers, gunnies, and ladies
of the night.

As the tall, black-haired man with the lake-blue
eyes guided his Ovaro stallion through the chill rain
and toward the lights of town, he realized that he was
glad he'd be sleeping in a warm, dry bed tonight. He'd
been six days traveling through the splendor of this
territory that included the rugged sight of the moun-
tains, which the glaciers had carved into breathtaking
peaks, gorges, and ravines. As he drove deeper toward
the plateau, timberlands as dense as he'd ever seen

appeared. Black walnut, Ponderosa pine, and Sitka spruce sprawled over the foothills.

The farmlands he eventually came to showed why so many hundreds of covered wagons had stopped when they reached the Willamette Valley here. It offered some of the most fertile lands in the entire west. The trail grew melancholy only as he neared the Indian reservation, where so many braves had been slaughtered at the behest of a mentally unbalanced Indian agent. Many different tribes now sang of the slaughter. The tragedy was one of legend among Indians of all tribes.

Cumberland, whose WELCOME sign boasted 7,423 souls, was the expected mixture of false fronts and one-story buildings. As his pinto sluiced through the muddy main street, Fargo noted that the buildings were well kept and that the board sidewalks on both sides of the street looked new. The telegraph office was open late as was the general store. Sure signs of prosperity.

Say what you might about betting parlors being havens for gamblers, they brought a lot of revenue into a town; revenue that benefited most of its citizens to some degree. But along with gambling came cardsharps, bunco artists of all stripes, and hoodlums.

Fargo found a livery where a middle-aged black man named James took one look at Fargo's horse and said, "Now that's a beautiful specimen."

"Thank you," Fargo replied.

"Yessir, I see just about every kind of equine there is. But I don't see one like this very often. I don't suppose he's for sale?"

"Afraid not."

"I got a standing order from Mister Clymer—gentleman who owns this livery—that if I ever see an outstanding piece of horseflesh, I'm to tell him right away. And this one here sure qualifies as an outstanding piece of horseflesh." He wore an old sweater, flannel shirt, work trousers. He talked around a corn cob pipe tucked deep into the corner of his mouth. His face and his voice conveyed a thoughtful intelligence.

"Well, I sure can't imagine selling him," Fargo said. "Not after all the things we've been through together."

Then he went looking for a hotel so he could take care of himself for the night.

He was surprised to find that two of the casinos were dark, their front doors padlocked. He was also surprised to see four elderly people wearing Amish-style hats parading in front of the Ruby Rooster, the only casino that was still open. They were chanting in some kind of protest.

> "Gambling is a sin . . .
> Satan works here . . .
> Gambling is shameful . . .
> The devil's den . . ."

The people leaving and entering the casino didn't pay any attention to the protesters. Apparently, this was a regular occurrence, the placard-carrying people paying the casino a nightly visit.

Fargo went on to the nearest hotel. It wasn't fancy, but it looked clean and felt warm. So he walked up to the desk and got himself a room for the night.

The beefy clerk with the boozy nose sneezed, sliding a finger beneath his nose as he did so. The finger turned suddenly green. He looked at the green stuff, and Fargo looked at the green stuff. Then the clerk wiped his finger off on his trouser leg and smiled as if nothing at all had happened. "Guess you'll be wanting a room," he said.

"Guess so." Fargo replied.

"Well, Lord knows there's nothing better than a dry bed on a wet and cold night."

"Yeah," Fargo said. "Say, I noticed that two of the casinos are closed. What happened?"

"Oh, it's a long story." The clerk obviously didn't want to talk about it.

"Those protesters have anything to do with it?"

He shrugged. "Sort of."

"Somebody should shoot those bastards," a man in a derby said from an armchair where he was reading the newspaper. "I used to come to Cumberland to have myself some fun. Me and a lot of other drummers. Now the only casino left is the Ruby Rooster. I don't know how much longer it can hold out, either."

"What's going on here?" Fargo said.

The derby man said, "Like Earl here says, it's a long story, mister."

Fargo hefted his saddlebags. "My room ready?"

"Should just about be," Earl said. "I got Doris the maid up there now. We're full up. We don't usually rent out that room. That's the way Doris wants it."

"I suppose if I ask you why you don't rent it out you'll tell me it's a—"

"—long story."

Instead of being sinister, the reluctance to talk was actually funny. Fargo expected hotel people to be talkers. That's what people did in hotels. Talked. Drank a little, sure. Had some sex if they were lucky enough, sure. But mostly they talked. Especially desk clerks and drummers. But Fargo got the sense that these two had talked so much about the subject that they were tired of it. It was just too damned boring to walk back through again.

Fargo headed upstairs.

The carpeting in the hallway was clean. The sconces were covered for safety. Somebody had sprinkled some nice-smelling stuff all over the walls. This was a good place to stay.

When he opened the door to Room 107, he saw a small but supremely well-fashioned blonde girl using a feather duster on the top of a bureau. She was singing to herself in a sweet, slightly off-key feminine voice, a sentimental mountain song, and apparently didn't hear him open the door. So he stood for a moment enjoying the view, the nicely rounded curve of buttock outlined against the dungaree bottom and the thrust of breast against the white cotton blouse.

When she became aware of him she smiled and said, "You're a big one." She didn't look startled at all. She had a country girl kind of composure he liked right away.

"You should see my horse," Fargo said, coming into the room. "I mean, if you think I'm big."

He dropped his saddlebags on the floor and walked over to the window. There was a shadowy alley below and a fog was settling on the rooftops of small houses in the distance.

"There you go," the girl said, using the duster one last time. "I put it all back together again."

"The clerk downstairs said there was something special about this room. And now you say that you put it all back together again. Something happened here?"

She shrugged. She had one of those sweet small-town faces that just made you feel good to look at. "Well, it's kind of—"

He laughed and stuck out a halting hand. "Don't say it."

"Don't say what?"

"That it's a long story."

"Well, actually, it kind of is."

"Well, I've got plenty of time on my hands, so let me hear it. And then let me ask you a couple of other questions, too . . . Any beer in this hotel?"

"There's a saloon downstairs."

"Good. Why don't you go get us some beer, and then you can tell me all about this room and this town. Say—are you old enough to drink beer?"

"I sure am. And I drink beer all the time, for your information. I'm nineteen."

"My name's Skye Fargo."

"Mine's Doris Mallory."

"Well, Doris Mallory, you go get us some beer and then you come back here and we'll talk. How about that?"

She smiled. There was just the slightest hint of sexuality in her expression. "You sure are a big one. And that's how I like 'em, I guess." The smile was wider now. "Big."

"Nobody was sure where she came from," Doris told Skye over a bucket of beer twenty minutes later. "Just showed up one day along about four months ago. Everybody fell in love with her. She was one of the most beautiful girls I ever saw. She worked over at the Ruby Rooster and had this room right here in the hotel. She was a dance girl but never a prostitute. She got to be as big a draw at the casino as the gambling."

"And what happened to her?"

"Killed herself. Right here in this room. I was the one who found her."

"You sure she killed herself?"

"Well, Skye, it sure looked that way. She had the gun next to her head. The wound was right above her temple."

"Why would a beautiful young girl kill herself?"

"I don't know," Doris said, tears gleaming in her eyes. "And it was kinda selfish of her is the way I feel. She always said I was the best friend she had in the whole world. I helped her do a lot of things— helped her get a horse, took her over to the bank and introduced her to Neil Anderson so she could open up her safety box, even tried to fix her up with some of the more respectable men around here."

"Did she go out with any of them?"

"No. That was the funny thing about her. You'd expect her to really enjoy herself, the way she looked and all. But she didn't. She didn't laugh much, for one thing. She was always real intense, like she had somethin' on her mind she wasn't lettin' you know about."

"So you didn't have any hint that she was going to kill herself?"

"Not at all. I know it's selfish—but the least she could've done was leave me a note."

No other series has this much historical action!

THE TRAILSMAN

#225:	PRAIRIE FIRESTORM	0-451-20072-1
#226:	NEBRASKA SLAYING GROUND	0-451-20097-7
#227:	NAVAJO REVENGE	0-451-20133-7
#228:	WYOMING WAR CRY	0-451-20148-5
#229:	MANITOBA MARAUDERS	0-451-20164-7
#230:	FLATWATER FIREBRAND	0-451-20202-3
#231:	SALT LAKE SIREN	0-451-20222-8
#235:	FLATHEAD FURY	0-451-20298-8
#237:	DAKOTA DAMNATION	0-451-20372-0
#238:	CHEROKEE JUSTICE	0-451-20403-4
#239:	COMANCHE BATTLE CRY	0-451-20423-9
#240:	FRISCO FILLY	0-451-20442-5
#241:	TEXAS BLOOD MONEY	0-451-20466-2
#242:	WYOMING WHIRLIND	0-451-20522-7
#243:	WEST TEXAS UPRISING	0-451-20504-9
#244:	PACIFIC POLECOATS	0-451-20538-3
#245:	BLOODY BRAZOS	0-451-20553-7
#246:	TEXAS DEATH STORM	0-451-20572-3
#247:	SEVEN DEVILS SLAUGHTER	0-451-20590-1
#248:	SIX-GUN JUSTICE	0-451-20631-2

To order call: 1-800-788-6262